"Are you su right guy?

Katie stopped blue gaze seeming to penetrate his soul. "Oh, yeah, I'm sure."

Mitch could hardly contain himself. All he wanted to do was push back from the table, lead her back to her hotel room and continue what they'd started the day before. He wanted her more than any woman he'd ever known. If he wasn't careful, he'd end up on his knees, begging her to stay with him. Because she was leaving. Tomorrow.

The band started up, and Katie smiled at him. "I never asked whether you could dance," she said. "Can you?"

The long list of high school dances that neither of them had attended echoed through his memory. He'd never asked Katie to a school dance because that would have been a connection, a starting point for the two of them. And also because he'd thought a smart girl like her would have stayed clear of the hell-raiser he'd been.

"That all depends," he said, getting to his feet. "Are you ready to show me off to your friends?"

Katie laughed. "I don't suppose I could talk you into doing a striptease?" she asked wickedly.

Mitch gave her a sly grin. "For you, Katie, anytime..."

Dear Reader,

Sweet Talkin' Guys... Yes, we've all known one. He's the guy who saunters into your life, making it his mission to tease you, provoke you and ultimately steal your heart. His weapons are his wit, his charm and his audaciousness—usually accompanied by a devastating smile. And sometimes he doesn't even have to say a thing....

Mitch McKee is one of those guys. He's not only a sweet-talker, he's Southern, which adds another layer of sugarcoating to his drawl. But this man, like all true heroes, isn't just a talker. He stands up for the people he loves, and steps back when he knows that getting what he wants might hurt someone else. He's a bad boy gone right...until sexy Katie Sutherland, the woman he let walk away from him years before, comes back into his life. Then it's a race to see who'll end up branded as the town hellion!

I hope you enjoy reading *Drop-Dead Gorgeous*. I had a great time writing it.

Happy reading,

Lyn Ellis

P.S. I'd love to hear from you. Write to me at P.O. Box 441, Bowie, MD 20720

DROP-DEAD GORGEOUS
Lyn Ellis

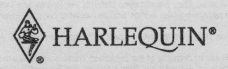

HARLEQUIN®

TORONTO • NEW YORK • LONDON
AMSTERDAM • PARIS • SYDNEY • HAMBURG
STOCKHOLM • ATHENS • TOKYO • MILAN • MADRID
PRAGUE • WARSAW • BUDAPEST • AUCKLAND

To my own Sweet Talkin' Guy—GMH
May the blarney never fail ye.
You make my heart happy. :))

ISBN 0-373-25881-X

DROP-DEAD GORGEOUS

Copyright © 2000 by Gin Ellis.

Visit us at www.eHarlequin.com

Printed in U.S.A.

1

CHIEF OF POLICE Mitch McKee had almost made it to the city limits of Chapel, Tennessee, when he overheard the radio call. He'd been trying to get out of town all evening to end one of the longer political days of his law enforcement career. A small college town outside Chattanooga, Chapel boasted the unique combination of old money and former moonshiners as part of its history. In the present, Mitch thought of the venerable Chapel city council as a pack of mules too stubborn to be dragged into the future, and his patience for political rhetoric had deserted him sometime after lunch.

He'd rather be fishing.

The radio wouldn't be silent, however. "Les, a motorist reported a car in a ditch on Ravenswood Road," Myra, the dispatcher, said to the deputy on duty. "A damsel in distress," she added, with the inflection of a matchmaking aunt.

"I'm on the way," Les answered, sounding less than perturbed by the prospect of being helpful on a slow crime night.

Mitch, on the other hand, was trying to clear his mind of the day he'd spent arguing with one or another of the city council.

It seemed that when he'd taken the office of chief of police, he'd also been elected to the post of "bully in charge." But when it came right down to it, they expected him to toe the official line. They firmly believed in not upsetting the status quo.

They should have known better.

Sure, the infamous Mitch McKee of the past had grown out of his wildest ways, served in the marines with honor—except for a few stints in the brig—but when it came to following the rules...he'd only follow the ones he didn't consider stupid.

Mitch could hardly bear to think anymore about the mayor's proposal to change the speed limit on any road with a church to fifteen miles per hour, seven days a week. The mayor's rationale had been that even if the parishioners weren't in services, traffic should slow down to show the proper respect.

To clear his mind, Mitch decided to give Les a hand with his "damsel." Ravenswood Road was on his way home, anyway. And, if he ended up pushing a car out of the mud, well, even that would be better than pushing another kind of load belonging to Mayor John Dealey. Mitch dreaded the thought of their next meeting. He himself might be a sinner, but at least he understood the concept of the phrase, "traffic flow."

FIFTEEN MINUTES LATER, Mitch shined his flashlight along several feet of skid marks ground into the asphalt of Ravenswood Road and shook his head.

"Are you training to drive for NASCAR, or what?"

he asked the well-dressed redhead currently sitting on the driver's-side door of her capsized gold Mercedes.

He'd already asked about her health, now he felt like it was his duty to discuss her driving since his deputy might have to issue a ticket.

"I'm an excellent driver," the woman sniffed. "I happened to be talking on my cell phone when a deer ran out in front of me."

"That's understandable, cell phones are lethal weapons. But from the looks of these tire marks you should have been talking to an air traffic controller. Lady, you must have been flyin' low."

The lady in question shifted her position on the car and crossed a pair of legs that made Mitch want to throw a blanket over them so he wouldn't be distracted. There was something familiar about her, but he doubted he'd met her before. If he had, he wouldn't have forgotten those legs.

"There's no need to bother with me," the redhead continued. "I've called my father's mechanic to give me a tow."

My father's mechanic. The smooth, utterly confident tone of her voice slid over him. He squinted to see her face better in the shifting light. That's when Mitch remembered her, and her pedigree. Katie Sutherland, the youngest daughter of the richest family in Chapel, Tennessee. The grown-up version of the young girl Mitch had managed to keep his hands off of when they'd been in high school, but just barely. He'd rarely heard her speak then. Now it seemed she'd learned to use her voice quite effectively.

Damn.

Mitch looked at Les, the deputy who'd officially taken the accident call, and shook his head. Terence Sutherland's daughter. Of all the females in the world... He returned his attention to the lady in question.

"Sorry about that, Ms. Sutherland, but we have to write up a report and I think we'll also have to give you a sobriety test."

"You can't be serious."

As he expected, she sounded indignant. "Sorry, ma'am, it's the law, and I'm the man in Chapel who enforces it. But first, one of us has to get you out of there."

"I prefer to stay where I am until Ramey arrives."

"I'll take that into consideration," Mitch said, then faced Les. "Since I'm already on my way home, and dressed for it, I guess I'll have to get muddy. But I'm ordering you to do the sobriety test."

"Whatever you say, Chief," Les said.

With a disgusted look at his favorite work boots, Mitch stepped off the pavement and made his way down to the churned up mud. When he reached his objective and he could see her better, he wanted to swear again. The young beauty who'd watched him throughout his senior year with wide-eyed curiosity, and who'd supplied the fuel for more than a few of his own testosterone fantasies, had grown into a true heartbreaker. Before he got all caught up in the new

Katie, however, she turned her head, doing her best to ignore him. In general, he'd always been pretty hard to ignore when he put his mind to it. Without waiting for permission, he slid an arm behind her and one under those impressive legs and lifted.

She squirmed in his grasp. "I told you I wanted to stay here. I could have you up on charges of sexual harassment. Put me down!"

"No. I'll note your disagreement in the report," he said as he took careful steps up the slope. "If it's against the law to carry a woman out of a mud hole, then the crime will just have to be attributed to my upbringing. My mother always said, 'Never leave a woman in the mud.'" Without acknowledging his deputy's laugh, Mitch continued, "Why did you dye your hair red?" Years ago she'd been a brunette.

"How did you know—" She leaned away from him in order to get a good look at his face. He felt her muscles clench as if he'd startled her. She didn't say a word.

"Now that's familiar. I remember anytime I tried to talk to you in school, you'd clam up. You don't have to worry now, though, I'm completely respectable. No more truant officers or juvenile court. Hell, your daddy helped get me elected chief of police."

"My *father*—" she pushed out of his grasp like a scalded cat just as they reached the pavement "—hasn't got the brains God gave a flea."

Mitch rubbed his chin concentrating on a comeback rather than the way his body had reacted to having her in his arms. "Let me get this straight, are you insulting him—" he grinned "—or me?"

Kate didn't know whether to throw her hands up in frustration or sit down on the pavement and cry. Mitch McKee. Why did she have to run into Mitch McKee? She'd intended to use her well-bred anonymity to charm the deputy so she wouldn't be ticketed for her own stupidity. Now that opportunity was ruined. Mitch had been her first and most out-of-control crush in school. She'd spent hours writing his name in her diary, slipping into the senior wing just to get a glimpse of him, watching him stand out in the parking lot with the other "bad" boys smoking at lunchtime. But she'd also felt completely humiliated each time he'd spoken to her and she'd stood there, speechless, with her heart beating like it had gotten stuck in her throat.

And now look at him. Drop-dead gorgeous even wearing jeans and muddy boots when he should have looked dirty. Had there ever been a time when she hadn't been overwhelmed by Mitch McKee?

Well, she'd have to show him she'd grown up.

"I'm insulting both of you, I suppose, if you've climbed into the same political bed."

Mitch looked slightly surprised. "Whoa, whoa." He raised a large hand to punctuate his words. "I didn't say anything about beds."

"Trust me, if my father helped you, then that's where he expects you to be." When he looked a little green around the gills at the thought, Kate relented slightly. She winked at Deputy Les. "That's figuratively speaking of course," she added.

The roar of the approaching tow truck caused the three of them to look toward the headlights. Mitch spoke first. "I'll make sure he doesn't damage your car anymore than it is. Les," he said to his deputy, "get started with the Breathalyzer so Miz Sutherland can go home."

"Wait just a minute—"

Mitch turned back to her and propped his hands on his hips. In that moment, he was one hundred percent, undiluted cop. "If you want a lawyer, then use your cell phone to call one. Otherwise, take the test, fill out the forms and be on your way. When you wreck a fifty-thousand dollar car, someone has to write it down."

Unable to settle on what to say first, Kate pushed her way past the deputy toward his police cruiser. She'd take their stupid test. She hadn't been drinking, she'd been crying. There was no law against that. And as far as wrecking the car...she didn't care. Her father would buy ten cars as long as she stayed out of his new perfect life. She just might take him up on it, too.

Since his boots were already muddy, Mitch helped Ramey, the tow truck driver, hook up the Mercedes. Old Ramey looked like he'd been dragged out of bed by his wife. Kate's little racing accident was getting on everyone's nerves. Mitch glanced at her just as she presented Les with her driver's license. She acted more mad then inebriated, except for the crack about him being in bed with her father. Some of that country club humor, no doubt.

He realized he'd forgotten to look for a wedding ring. Was her name still Sutherland? Had she moved out to San Francisco, married some guy named Chad or Brad and put the dust of tiny, backwoods Chapel, Tennessee, behind her? He couldn't blame her if she had. He'd done much the same by staying in the military after Judge Wrensdale had ordered him to join or go to jail for car theft. He'd wanted to put this town and everything in it out of his thoughts. But he'd never managed to put the memory of Katie's fragile face behind him. Especially the way she'd looked the first time she'd come back to school after her mother died. She'd been all eyes and sadness.

As he walked up to the police car, he could hear Les explaining the sobriety test to her. Mitch arrived at the open passenger side of the car, just as Les spoke.

"Okay, now blow."

As Kate followed instructions, Mitch felt the blood leaving his face, moving downward. The embarrassment of his body's reaction to the sight of Kate's lips wrapped around a piece of diagnostic equipment made him turn and walk away again. But not before he saw Kate roll her eyes at him.

He felt like kicking the side of the patrol car as he walked back to his own four-wheel drive. Did she ascertain what a complete pervert he'd turned into? *Come on, Mitch, you've seen belly dancers suck snakes before—what has happened to you?* He could only attribute his reaction to the shock of seeing the sweet young Katie from his past transformed into this grown-up, and very sexy Katie. Like finding out the little girl next door has become a Playboy Bunny while you weren't looking, yet being unable to drag your gaze from the centerfold.

But Kate hadn't posed nude or even looked at him suggestively. All she'd done was take the sobriety test he'd ordered her to take.

"Chief?"

Mitch looked up to see Les walking toward him.

"Miz Sutherland didn't register any numbers. She's clean."

"Okay, let's get her on her way." Mitch wanted to be on his way as well. Too many conflicts of interest in this situation. The past running into the present. Playboy colliding with a high-school yearbook.

"I'd like to thank you, deputy, for being so sensible about not giving me a ticket," Kate said.

Mitch leveled a dark gaze at Les and the man had the sense to look nervous. Kate deserved a ticket, but Mitch wasn't going to press the issue.

Les touched his hat and nodded. "We're all glad you weren't hurt, ma'am. Thanks for your help, Chief," he added before making a beeline for his cruiser. Mitch watched him drive away before he spoke again.

"I thought you moved out to California."

"I did." Her gaze was on the tow truck as Ramey tightened down the ties on her car.

Since she didn't elaborate, he changed the subject. "Your car looks trashed."

Her expression remained neutral. She seemed pre-occupied now that the excitement was over. "Oh, I don't know, a few dents give it character, don't you think?"

After the size of that understatement, Mitch could only stare at her. Maybe she'd lost a few of her marbles during one of those California earthquakes. Her car wasn't going to be rolling anywhere for a while, character or not. There were no rental-car offices in Chapel, Tennessee. So, he decided to make the offer, even if she turned him down. "You'll need a ride back out to your father's place."

Something he said caused her features to change, and the tone of her voice hardened. "I'm not staying at my father's, nor am I staying at my sister's."

Thinking he was way out of his depth, he merely said, "Oh."

"I'm staying at my friend Julie's. Since your memory is so outstanding, do you remember Julie Taylor, now Julie Blake?"

"Yeah. I know the Blakes. Cal and I go fishin' whenever we get a chance." Then Mitch asked what he really wanted to know. "How long are you and your husband gonna be in town? It'll take awhile to get that car fixed."

"*I'll* be here at least until the class reunion this weekend," she answered. Then she changed the subject. "Are you going?"

Mitch winced a bit. Why would he go to her class

reunion when he hadn't gone to any of his own? "I graduated in a different class, remember?" The class of USMC.

Ramey was wiping his hands on a greasy rag as he approached them. It looked like he was finally ready to roll.

"What are you gonna do about getting another car?" Mitch asked again since she didn't seem to be registering her predicament. And his male programming wouldn't allow him to leave a problem unsolved. Katie Sutherland probably didn't want or need his help, but he was determined to give her the option. He was surprised by the cocky smile on her face when she turned to him, because he could also see the sparkle of tears in her eyes.

"Why, I'll get Daddy to buy me a new one."

Her words should have put him off, but for some reason they did the opposite. Mitch took her arm and nudged her toward his four-wheel drive. "Come on, I'll take you over to Julie's."

When she pulled back slightly, he added, "My truck will be easier on your clothes than Ramey's. I didn't save you from the mud to have you look like you've been out secretly working on diesel engines for a hobby." He watched her calculate exactly how much grease Ramey actually had on his overalls, then allowed Mitch to open his passenger door for her.

The first few miles were traveled in silence. After giving in to his offer, Kate seemed to sag into the seat. He figured the reality of the accident had finally sunk in. He let her be for the moment, thinking of how many times in high school he'd watched her. He'd let her be then too, and look where that had gotten them.

"It's been a long time since high school," he said, thinking out loud.

Kate sniffed once before pushing herself up straighter in the seat. She turned toward him slightly. "It has," she stated the obvious. Then she surprised him by asking, "How have you been? I thought you'd joined the marines." It sounded like a platitude but the tone of her voice was genuine.

He glanced at her to see if she was baiting him, but she seemed to be waiting for his answer.

"I've been fine—good," he said then chuckled at the stupidity of the answer. "I've done well. Not as well as you, I would imagine." He shrugged. "Spent some time getting my butt kicked into shape in the military, then the brass asked me to do a little work in the desert. I survived it. Came home and became one of Chapel's model citizens." He chuckled again at how that sounded.

"Chief of police," she said.

"Yeah," he said and frowned. "It has turned out to be more politics than police work, and I'm not sure I like that scenario. But I took the job and I'll do it."

"Your mother must be proud," she said.

Surprised that she would remember his mother, he answered her honestly. "I think she was. I'm glad I could do something to make her proud, after all the trouble I caused way back when. She did her best, but without my father to help, she couldn't keep me in line. I thought I knew better than she did about how I should grow up. And I was taller than her." The image of his tiny mother looking up at him and giving him dire warnings about his future if he didn't toe the line nearly made him smile. He hesitated, but he knew he had to tell Kate the rest. "She died two years ago."

"I'm sorry, I didn't know—"

"No need to be sorry. You've been gone a long time, no reason to be keeping up with the folks back home."

Forced to stop at a red light, Mitch turned and met Kate's gaze. She seemed sadder still and he had the urge to drive to somewhere cheerful, a diner maybe, where they could have a cup of coffee and a piece of pie and talk until she smiled.

"How have you been?" he asked instead.

"Oh, I've been—" she looked out the window to watch a car pass "—fine."

She'd mimicked his words but didn't seem ready to elaborate. He went for the easy stuff. "I heard you got some kind of big job out in San Francisco."

Kate glanced back at him with a slight smile on her face. "If by *big* you mean well-paid, then I'm guilty as charged."

He started the truck forward, regretting the light change. "Well, money isn't everything, I know, especially to someone who—"

"Was born with so much of it?" Kate finished for him. "Is that what you mean?"

A buzz of irritation ran through Mitch. "No, that's not what I mean. Not exactly. I know about your family, and yes, that gives you a little edge over some others. What I'm talking about is whether or not you like what you get paid so much to do."

"I do like it," Kate said, sounding less defensive.

"Great!" Mitch replied. "Now you want to tell me exactly what the he— heck it is?"

Kate smiled at his frustration and without warning he felt like he'd scored the winning touchdown at homecoming. A hero for getting her to smile when she'd been on the verge of tears.

"I'm a headhunter," she answered and he could hear the wisecracking tone in her voice.

"Excuse me?"

"Some of the largest corporations in the country hire our firm to find the best and the brightest employees to fill their requirements."

"I see. And how do you find the best and brightest?"

"We recruit at the top colleges, have a Web site on the Net and we raid other companies. It makes me feel like a shark sometimes."

"That's a far cry from anything that happens in the sleepy town of Chapel. No wonder you love it." Mitch said, thinking about how he'd intended to get out of Chapel and never come back. Now that his mother was gone, there was nothing holding him here. "Maybe you could find me a job." He was only half-joking. The joking part was including himself in her description of the best and the brightest.

"Don't you like the one you have?" she asked.

He thought about that for a moment. He liked law

enforcement, but his job as chief was... "Not very exciting," he said aloud as they pulled up in front of Cal and Julie's.

Kate turned to him as he shut the engine off. "Thank you for the ride, Chief," she said, mimicking his deputy's tone. She opened her door and stepped out of the truck before he could react. "And about your job not being very exciting...you might want to be careful what you wish for. Good night."

2

THE NEXT MORNING, dressed in designer sweats and a cropped T-shirt, Kate faced her friend across the kitchen table and a half-empty coffee cup.

"Oh, Julie, what am I going to do?"

Julie, who was rapidly approaching seven months of pregnancy, had the nerve to laugh.

"The way I see it, there's nothing you need to do other than get on with your life. Driving more carefully would be a good thing as well."

"I should have never come back to this town," Kate sighed. "I thought something might have changed up there on the hill. That maybe my father..."

Julie shifted to find a more comfortable spot on the chair. "You know, I just don't understand you," she said. "You should be settled down and starting a family of your own rather than trying to please the King of the Hill. You've been working on him for years and it hasn't changed his attitude. And now..."

Kate stared at her friend and felt the heat of tears rising in her eyes. Yeah, she'd done everything she could to be the daughter her father might be proud of. The problem was, however, no matter how many scholarships she'd gotten for school, no matter what kind of high-powered job she'd landed, she could never be the child he'd be proud of. Because now he had a son.

Kate picked up her napkin and wiped her eyes. "I know. And I know how neurotic this looks. But since I lost my mom, he's all I've got, he and Carrie. I feel like if I hang on, he might have a change of heart."

"Don't take offense," Julie said, "but I'm not sure the man has a heart. After everything you've done to prove yourself? Heck, you'll see what I mean at the reunion on Saturday night. You've sprinted past everyone in your class and your hometown. You've been rubbing elbows with the rich and richer in San Francisco, you have a job with a salary that makes every man in this town grit his teeth, and you look like your face should be on the cover of a magazine. The rest of us girls—" she patted her stomach "—have been stayin' home and having babies."

"For all the good it's done me with my father, I might as well have run away from home and lived on the wild side instead." Kate watched her friend's features go impish.

"Well, it's never too late to start," Julie said.

"What in the world are you talking about?"

"Well..." Julie leaned closer and motioned for Kate to do the same. "Being the bad girl in town sounds like a lot more fun than marching to the beat of your father's drummer. He's not even paying attention. You're over the legal age of consent. Maybe it's time to get wild."

When Kate couldn't find an answer, Julie continued, "Oh, I wish I wasn't as big as a whale. I'd love to help you rock this town."

"Rock the town?" Kate repeated stupidly. "Why would I want to do that?"

"Because Chapel, Tennessee, doesn't recognize Kate Sutherland. They only see Terrence Sutherland's daughter. So whatever you do will be directly relayed to him." Julie sat back with a self-satisfied smile and placed a hand on her protruding belly. "I only wish I could be a fly on the wall..." Julie didn't hesitate. "Okay, get out your pocket planner and we'll make a list."

"Of what?"

Julie gave Kate a devilish look then waggled her eyebrows. "A list of the things bad girls do."

Bad girls. Kate would've given anything to have been a bad girl back in high school. She hadn't envied their freedom, or even their seeming disdain for authority. She'd envied their access to the students on the fringe, their uninhibited ability to talk to and even flirt with the notorious Mitch McKee.

"Are you listening to me?" Julie asked.

"Not really," Kate answered, then smiled at Julie's affronted look. "I was thinking about Mitch. It was a shock to see him last night."

"I bet." Julie laughed. "Looks even better than he did in high school, doesn't he?"

Better? No, Kate decided, not better. More dangerous would be closer to the mark. Being in his arms, even for a short time and a mundane reason had taken her breath away. Had made her feel like he'd grown up and she'd remained seventeen. "He looks great," Kate answered in a bored manner. No use fueling those fires again.

"You know, Mitch might be able to help you with this bad girl thing. He's certainly known his share," Julie went on.

"Not a good idea." For a thousand reasons. "He and my father seem to be big buddies now. I doubt he'd want to cross him on my behalf." For some reason the thought of Mitch aligning himself with her father made her more determined. The only two men she'd ever wanted desperately to impress had looked right past her.

It was enough to make any sane woman go bad.

Outside a car horn blew and Kate walked to the window. On the street was a brand-new gold Mercedes. The dealer was delivering a new car for her to use while she was in town—paid for by her father. She might not have his heart, but she certainly had his wallet, as long as she didn't cause any trouble. That's when something coiled up inside Kate seemed to relax. She'd already put one car in a ditch, that was a start. She gathered her girlish memories of Mitch as her hero and banished them to the place they'd been hidden for ten years. Then she turned to Julie with a smile. "You know what? I'm going to find out if you're right. Let's see how my father likes having a twenty-eight-year-old delinquent for a daughter."

"SHE DID WHAT?" Mitch said into the phone. Al, the owner of the local diner, was speaking so fast Mitch didn't know if he could trust his ears.

"That Kate Sutherland brought Old Henry and sat him down in my restaurant in the middle of the lunch rush. She told him to order anything he wanted and now she's waiting while he eats it. She *instructed* me to send her father the bill. Hell, I'm probably losing two hundred dollars worth of business—you know how that old wino smells!"

Mitch did indeed know how aromatic Old Henry could be. He'd had him in jail often enough to sleep off a bender. "Well, you know, Al, buying somebody lunch isn't really illegal."

"I say she's disturbing the peace—my peace—and my right to do business and I—"

"I'll talk to her, Al. But I can't have her arrested. If I did then she might come back at you with a discrimination suit."

"I have a right to discriminate when someone puts me out of business. I'm going to call Terry Sutherland and just see what he thinks should be done."

That sounded like a vague threat but Mitch wasn't too concerned. He hung up the phone thinking that Terry Sutherland needed to turn his daughter over his knee and settle this with corporal punishment. He had a feeling words weren't gonna do it with Kate. They hadn't the evening before when he'd carried her out of a ditch. But he would try again in any case. He reached for his keys and went out to find the perpetrator.

He found her just where Al had said he would, sitting in a booth across from Old Henry with her back to the front windows as if she intended to face down every person in the restaurant. As Mitch walked through the door he couldn't help but notice that the booths and tables around Kate and Henry were conspicuously vacant. A reluctant wave of admiration ran through him for her spunk.

Al met him at the door. "You see what I'm talking about?" Al asked. He had tried to keep his voice down to a loud whisper but even so, a few people turned to the sound. Kate was one of those people. When her eyes met Mitch's, she seemed to freeze.

"Did you call Terry Sutherland?" Mitch asked without taking his gaze from Kate's. He'd rather have her father deal with her since she had the uncanny effect of reverting his libido back to high-school levels. At the advanced age of thirty he didn't need to get *that* excited.

"He said to let you handle it."

Mitch looked at Al. "He did, did he?" *Damn.* Why couldn't the man deal with his own family problems? Not that he considered what Kate was up to a bona fide problem. She wasn't robbing a bank or anything.

"Like I told you, Al, I can't arrest her for buying someone lunch—even if it is Old Henry."

"Well, you're the chief of police, you can go talk to her."

Mitch could see Al wasn't going to give up until he did. As he approached the booth where Kate had taken up residence, she turned her attention back to the old man.

"Did you have enough dessert? Want another piece of pie?"

Without asking permission, Mitch pulled a chair from an adjacent table, turned it backward to the booth and sat down propping his arms on the seat back.

"Well, hello, Kate. Henry." He nodded.

Mitch McKee. Kate had to concentrate on her breathing so she wouldn't hyperventilate. *How can he still do this to me after all these years?* It didn't make sense. She'd had dinner at the White House, danced with the Governor of California and been to parties with real movie stars in the room. And Mitch McKee could still stun her speechless.

In the dark the night before, he hadn't been quite as imposing—perhaps because she'd been so upset. But now, with his broad shoulders blocking any escape from the booth, she felt overwhelmed.

Kate watched as Henry put down his fork guiltily, and something about that action fired her indignance.

"You go ahead and finish your pie, Henry," she said. Then she defiantly faced Mitch. "There's no law against eating in a public place."

When Henry continued to stare at Mitch waiting for permission, he nodded. "That's right, there isn't. Finish your pie." The old man picked up his fork again. "What are you up to?" Mitch asked Kate.

"I thought Henry needed a good meal."

"Yes, and I would agree with you but there are other ways to do this. The church provides—"

"I thought Henry had a right to eat in this restaurant just like any other citizen of this town." She looked past Mitch and gave Al, her father's friend, her best evil eye. Bringing Henry to the diner didn't really count as "dating the wrong men," as she and Julie had put on her bad girl to-do list, but it was a start. She couldn't smoke in a nonsmoking area. Swearing didn't seem appropriate for a family restaurant. So she'd commandeered Old Henry. It had certainly given Al indigestion.

When she returned her attention to Mitch, he had a calculating look on his face. "This isn't about Henry, is it?"

Kate felt like he'd just gazed through her head and read all her hopes, fears, and motives. She'd stood her ground face-to-face with CEOs from some of the biggest companies in the world. There was something about Chief of Police Mitch McKee, however, that made her lose focus. But she wasn't going to give in so easily.

"What do you mean? Of course, it's about Henry. He's lived in this town since before I was born and—"

"Hold it," Mitch stopped her. "I know the history of this town. I grew up here too, remember?"

Boy, did she remember, Kate fumed. During school her constellation revolved around the sun of Mitch. But things were different now. She couldn't sit back and be the "nice" girl. The quiet girl. The sad girl. "I know you did, but obviously you've gotten complacent about some of the things that go on here. Like my father..."

Mitch didn't say a word; he didn't have to. She'd said the wrong thing and could see it on his face. Bingo.

"What does your father have to do with this?"

"Nothing," Kate replied, trying to find a way to salvage the situation. "He and Al are such big buddies I thought Al wouldn't mind if I came in here to treat Henry."

"I see," Mitch said, holding her gaze.

Kate felt transfixed, as if everyone in the restaurant had disappeared, leaving her and Mitch to spar verbally to their hearts' content without an audience. Her face felt hot and her palms tingled at the prospect.

In the moment of silence that followed, reality intruded. Old Henry spoke up. "Can I go now?"

Mitch took over then. He stood and backed the chair out of the old man's way. "Sure."

Henry looked at Kate and said a brief thank-you before hightailing it out the door as fast as a crippled old man could move.

"You're lucky you didn't give him a heart attack," Mitch said as he sat back down.

"How could I have done that?" Kate asked.

"You know, he has his routines, his friends, people who look out after him. Then you bring him into the center of the town's power structure and expect him to calmly eat lunch across from the daughter of the town's leading citizen who, by the way—" his gaze made a leisurely trail along her bare arm, to her waist, down her hip, to her knees "—looks like a fashion model." Mitch shook his head and gazed at her. "That kind of attention could even put a strain on my heart."

At the word heart, Kate's attention dropped to the center of Mitch's khaki shirt and she couldn't help but wonder who'd had the privilege of feeling his heart beat in the years she'd been away. Unfortunately, that preoccupation left her with no interesting or witty comeback to his statement. Tongue-tied as usual when it came to Mitch McKee, Kate decided discretion had to be the better part of valor. She'd accomplished her mission—her first attempt at disobedience had gone well unless you counted not being arrested.

"May I go now?" she asked Mitch.

Mitch hesitated for a long and nerve-wracking minute. "Are you sure there isn't something I can help you with?" he asked. "I'm a pretty good listener."

Not wanting him to know how much that offer meant, she kept her mind on the goal. She didn't need help. She needed to show her father a thing or two. She had plans.

"I assure you, I'm perfectly fine." She looked up as she saw Al approaching the table. "But you might need some backup to handle Al. Bye."

Mitch watched her walk through the restaurant along with most of the other patrons. Al was spouting some kind of nonsense about erecting a sign saying he had a right to refuse service, blah, blah, blah.

As Kate stepped out into the afternoon sunshine,

she turned for a moment and looked back at him. That one look telegraphed two sureties to Mitch. The first had to do with more trouble. He'd caused enough in the past to know the signs. Ms. Kate Sutherland had an agenda and even though Mitch didn't know what it was yet, he was sure he'd be the one who would have to deal with it. The other surety was purely personal, purely instinct. It had to do with sex. As of this moment, he and Kate had stepped into the metaphorical man-woman dance, and Mitch hadn't been a leading citizen long enough to be the one to say no this time.

3

"WHY DON'T YOU CALL HIM instead?" Carrie, Kate's sister, suggested. "You know Daddy hates surprise visits. They've got the baby on a strict schedule and—"

"We wouldn't want to upset the schedule," Kate interrupted, unable to hide her sarcasm. She didn't remember their mother having them abide by some set-in-stone list of rules. This had to be their father's idea on how to raise a child. "So, I should call my own father and make an appointment? Is that what you do?"

"Of course. Just showing up at someone's house is the height of bad manners."

"Even if you used to live in the house?" Kate's childhood memories, all the memories she had of her mother, were tied to the house her father now lived in with his new family. Suddenly, she and Carrie had become outsiders. Carrie had managed to get past her pride, play by his rules and stay in her father's good graces. Kate had moved away to make her mark on the world thinking her father would have to acknowledge her success. She'd been wrong. He might acknowledge her success but he wasn't going to invite her back into his life without an appointment.

"Doesn't it bother you that we aren't welcome in our own home?"

"That was our home a long time ago, Kate."

A lifetime ago.

Her sister had made her own peace with the Devil, a peace that Kate could neither understand nor support. That left them with little to talk about. Kate looked at her watch, needing an excuse. "Speaking of time, I guess I should be going." She stood and picked up her purse.

Carrie stopped her forward motion. "Are you positive you don't want me to call him and set something up?"

"No, I appreciate it but that's okay," Kate replied keeping her voice breezy and unconcerned. Carrie jumping at the chance to be the good daughter made Kate feel even worse for the two of them. "I'm sure he'll get around to me sooner or later." Especially if she made herself too hard to ignore. "I'll be at Julie's until Friday, then at the resort until Sunday if you want to get together."

"Do you have a date for the reunion?" Carrie asked, before Kate made it out the door.

"No, not yet. Since I had two dates during my whole high school experience, I'm not optimistic." Between her shyness and her mother's illness, she hadn't participated in most of the dating rituals of adolescence. In college, she'd been determined to stay on the Dean's list. She'd dated, but hadn't found anyone special. In her business life she was required to attend a certain number of social functions, but she'd usually gone with colleagues rather than Mr. Right hopefuls. That left her on her own and dateless for the reunion.

"Well, you could always ask Mitch McKee, he's single and, well, you know what I mean...eligible."

Kate could feel color rising to her face. She knew exactly what her sister meant. Mitch was the kind of flesh-and-blood man who could cause an eighty-year-old spinster's heart to pound. Hadn't she experienced that very feeling while sitting across the booth from him in the diner?

Carrie had known about her girlish crush on Mitch when they were in school; she'd found pages in Kate's notebook with his name scribbled all over them. Guilty as charged. She couldn't tell if Carrie was being friendly or trying to put her in her place with sarcasm. A Sutherland wouldn't seriously consider dating a man who'd nearly gone to jail—chief of police or not. Kate was willing to admit to her past, but she'd grown up and she wasn't in the mood for being teased about the equally grown-up and very eligible Mitch McKee.

"Maybe I will," she said bravely. "Wouldn't that give our father a case of indigestion?" Most definitely not, she vowed silently. If she was going to pull off this bad-girl plan she couldn't involve Mitch. He was the one element she couldn't control, the one person who could discombobulate her and ruin everything.

As she dug in her bag for her keys, she found the unopened pack of cigarettes she'd purchased at the minimart. Needing a diversion, she brought them out of her purse along with her keys.

Carrie immediately zeroed in on the pack. "I didn't know you'd started smoking," she said, as though Kate owed her an explanation.

Since Kate hadn't actually *started* smoking, she couldn't answer directly without lying outright. She went for the dodge. "There are a lot of things you don't know about me," she said, then slipped out the door with a wave.

"CHIEF? I got Les on the radio. Can you come and talk to him?" Myra the dispatcher rarely interrupted him for radio calls. Mitch had the unpleasant vision of a bad wreck, a murder in progress or something else his deputy couldn't handle. He left his office and hurried down the hall to the dispatcher's desk. He picked up the handheld mike and responded.

"Go ahead, Les, this is the chief."

"Chief? Listen, I, uh, I got a situation over here at the Shell station on Thompson Road." He paused then and Mitch waited listening to the static. "Well, I, uh..."

"Spit it out, Les."

"Do you remember the other night when Miz Sutherland put her car in the ditch?"

At the mention of Kate's name, Mitch's heart seemed to fall in his chest. Was she hurt? Was she...? "Yes, I remember. Tell me what's happened, Deputy." Mitch knew he rarely used that tone of voice on Les but he needed him to get to the point.

"Well, sir, she's down here at the station assaulting the soda machine."

"Would you say that again?" Mitch asked, since he couldn't really believe his ears. He heard Myra give a hoot of laughter.

"She's broken open the soda machine and she's giving the sodas to the Chapel Bombers. The Little League Team, sir."

Mitch knew he'd rattled his deputy because Les had never called him "sir" so many times in a row. He also knew his deputy was way out of his league when dealing with Kate Sutherland.

"I'll be right there," he said. "Make sure she stays put till I arrive."

"Oh, I don't think that'll be a problem, Chief. She just reared back to go at it again."

Mitch took one of the patrol cars so he could use the flashing lights and cut across traffic. He was beginning to think there might be something seriously weird about California if it could turn a shy, sweet girl like Katie into the kind of woman who would attack a soda machine. What the devil was she up to?

As he pulled into the station from the far side, the scene before him looked too comical to be true. He put the car in park and stepped out just as Kate, to the cheers of about twenty ten-year-olds, put another respectable dent in the beleaguered soda machine with a well-placed kick. The manager of the station, Bob, stood next to Les shaking his head. Katie hadn't seen Mitch pull up, and no one's life seemed in imminent danger so he allowed himself one long appreciative study of the way her jeans curved along her backside and the toned, but feminine, muscles in her arms. Almost tall enough to look him in the eye, she was enough to make him break out in a sweat. On the next windup, he stepped behind her and grabbed her arm.

"Hey!" she said, spinning to face him. Then, like always when she realized who he was, she went wide-eyed and silent. Her face, already red from the exertion of beating the soda machine into submission, grew a little pinker, and her hands, suddenly without purpose, nervously shoved hair out of her face. She looked like an avenging angel gone berserk and he could only wonder what could get her that riled up and passionate. He was about to find out.

"Kate, what do you think you're doing?"

She drew herself up straighter and pointed to the wounded machine. "That machine took their money." She nodded toward the team.

"So why didn't you get Bob to give it back?"

She crossed her arms and with a menacing glance, shrugged toward the station's manager. "He said they would have to get it from the soda company, he didn't own the machine. Now what kind of thing is that to tell these kids?"

"What kind of thing is this—" he pointed toward the damage on the machine "—to teach kids about dealing with anger?"

Kate looked really nervous then and she faced the boys. "I told you guys never to do this, didn't I? You know I'll have to pay for this machine, no matter how much it costs."

"Did you also tell them they could go to jail for vandalism and petty theft?"

Most of the boys stopped grinning and Kate lost most of her pinkness.

"You boys get your drinks and go along home," Mitch ordered. "Ms. Sutherland here will pay for them."

When the Little Leaguers started moving, Mitch called to his deputy. "Les, I want you to come over and arrest Ms. Sutherland. The charge is assault and battery on a soda machine." Everyone in the immediate vicinity stopped dead in their tracks. Bob started shaking his head harder as Les made his way toward them.

Kate turned to him in what looked like a mix of shock and satisfaction. "You're going to arrest me?"

"Yes, ma'am, I am." Mitch had to work to keep from giving himself away. He wasn't going to take her to jail, but he wanted these boys to see her in handcuffs. He knew how tempting small crime and petty theft could be to adolescent boys. He'd been there, done that. No use encouraging them. If Kate really wanted to help, then she needed to cooperate.

"Now, wait a minute, Chief. I never said I wanted her arrested," Bob argued, looking a little pale himself. "Her daddy is my boss and I—"

Kate was the one to answer. "Don't worry, Bob, you won't lose your job over this. I'll be sure and tell my father who decided to arrest me."

Mitch made a conscious decision not to look into her mesmerizing face. As sad as it was to say, her anger had a warming rather than a chilling effect. When he'd grabbed her arm and she'd whirled on him, the only thought in his head had been to pull her to him and kiss her, to feed the fire until he became the target. He could show her other ways to generate heat. He had to get a grip before she turned him back into the bad boy everyone knew he used to be.

"Turn around, please, ma'am," Deputy Les said and when she complied he began putting the cuffs on Kate's wrists.

Jamie, one of the Little Leaguers, came over to make one last plea. "Sir, please, don't take her to jail. She only did it for us."

Mitch put a hand on the boy's shoulder. "I know she did, but when you make a decision to break the law for whatever the reason, you have to pay the price. She'll be okay. I'll look out for her. Now go on home."

"I'm fine, Jamie," Kate said, sounding a little breathless. "It was a dumb idea. I shouldn't have gotten so angry."

"Put her in the back of my car," Mitch ordered Les. "Show her how to sit with handcuffs on." If anyone would have ever asked him to bet, he'd never have imagined having Kate Sutherland in handcuffs under arrest. As he watched her walk toward his car he decided he would have lost the bet big-time. Kate wasn't the type...until now.

Mitch waited and watched as the boys slowly dispersed. Deputy Les seemed to take an interminably long time to settle Kate in the car, and Bob's nervousness hadn't abated.

"She told me to bill her father for the machine," Bob said. "How am I gonna do that?"

"I guess you tell him the truth. If he doesn't want to pay for it, then you'll have to deal with the insurance company. I can book her for the record."

"No. I'll handle it. Have you ever seen such a thing?" He walked away still shaking his head.

After the hubbub died down, Mitch walked slowly to his borrowed cruiser and slid behind the wheel.

"That was a dumb thing to do, Kate."

"I know," she agreed. Her easy agreement surprised him. "I should have thought it through."

"You mean you thought at all?"

Answered by silence, he turned to look at her through the steel grating. She didn't seem cowed, just quiet. He wondered if she was planning something else.

"You haven't been dabbling in the drug culture out there in California, have you?"

That got her immediate and clear-eyed attention. "No, I have not. Why would you ask that?"

Mitch shook his head then left the car to open the back door where she'd been placed. He indicated for her to turn around so he could unlock the cuffs.

"Because I don't remember you being this wild in school. Hell, I feel like you and I have exchanged personalities. I used to be the rebellious one."

Kate looked up at him as she rubbed her wrists and her expression seemed pained. Sort of like the first night he'd seen her smiling with tears in her eyes. The quick mix of emotions made his chest tight.

"Have you got a cigarette?"

When he gave her a frown for an answer, she shrugged. "I found out that wild girls have more fun," she said simply, with none of the bravado a true wild girl would have.

The answer angered him for no apparent reason. He should have laughed. "Are you having fun now?" he asked, as he indicated the cuffs and the police cruiser.

"You bet. Am I free to go?"

"Sure, as long as you don't drive by the ballfield and give the team a high five."

She looked disappointed, and for the life of him, Mitch couldn't figure out why. He was letting her go, for cripes' sake.

"Thank you, Chief. I'm sure my father will appreciate the favor."

As he watched her walk away, he had the almost uncontrollable urge to catch up and shake her until she explained what was going on in that brilliant little mind. He hadn't really been serious about the drugs but he still hadn't hit on the reason Kate Sutherland seemed to have had a personality transplant. His fascination was for selfish reasons. The sweet, shy Katie from high school had been a temptation, but resistible. This new and passionate Kate might be impossible to stay away from. If she wanted to know wild, he could teach her wild, and they'd both probably never be the same.

4

KATE KNEW she should lie low the next day or so. Not because she had no mischief planned, mind you. No, she had plenty of things left on her list. She decided to lie low because she didn't want to have to deal with Mitch McKee again. He'd downright unnerved her when he'd gotten angry at her attack on the soda machine. If he hadn't let her go—in deference to her father, she was sure—she might have been impressed. Or, at least, cowed slightly. It reinforced the fact that she had no idea what to expect from Mitch. And no way to predict what part he might play in her plans.

He'd said he thought they'd switched personalities. It suddenly occurred to her that she had no notion why Mitch, himself, had been so rebellious in his youth. He'd certainly caused enough trouble to be noticed but, somehow, getting attention didn't seem to fit the Mitch McKee she knew. And he hadn't had a father like hers to rebel against.

She knew he must have thought she was acting like a child, but that was the whole point. Mitch, or Carrie, even Julie, would never completely understand. She had no other options in this pseudo-standoff with her father. If she didn't become unmistakably visible in

her father's life, then she might as well disappear altogether.

Forced to stop at a red light, Kate rubbed the back
of her too warm neck and wished for a draft of cool,
fog-laden air off the bay. She'd left San Francisco and
her controlled, if one-track life a mere three days before and already felt like an alien in her own skin.
Craziness must be in the water supply of Chapel,
Tennessee. If any of the partners in her firm had seen
Ms. Kathleen Sutherland, top recruiter in Grayson,
Chambers and Leontine, attacking a soda machine or
in handcuffs, they would have sworn it had to be her
evil twin.

Kate had never done anything so undignified or
destructive in her life, although she was beginning to
understand why people did such things. In the midst
of her attack, she'd felt a great satisfaction in taking
out her anger at her father on an inanimate object.

And Mitch. When he'd stopped her midswing,
she'd wanted to pound on his chest in frustration. For
a split second, as she'd stared into his challenging
eyes, he'd no longer been the intimidating Mitch
McKee. She'd simply wanted to respond—to scratch
and bite, and kiss.

Mitch had made her feel like a woman to be reckoned with. That is until he'd fallen in step with the
rest of this small town, which her father practically
owned, and let the name Sutherland slide by his con-
victions. Kate wished he'd put her in jail. Next time,
she'd make sure he did. She hoped she wouldn't have
to shoot somebody to get his attention.

She parked the loaner Mercedes on the street in front of the Blakes', and found Julie waiting for her at the front door.

"Well? What happened?"

As Julie fussed over her like a prizefighter in training, Kate sat down with a glass of soda and told her "coach" about the incident at the Shell station. Julie seemed duly impressed until Kate tried to explain how Mitch treated her.

"Okay, you say he was mad, but he let you go?" Julie asked, a perplexed look on her face. "I know Mitch can be intimidating but I don't think I could say I've ever seen him really angry. How could you tell?"

Kate thought back and pictured Mitch frowning over her claim of being a wild girl. The way his voice lowered and tensed as he asked her, *Are you having fun now?* He'd sounded like he thought she wasn't supposed to have fun, or be wild. The pot calling the kettle black.

"I don't know, I could just tell."

"Well, not to worry," Julie said patting Kate on the knee. "We have more things on our to-do list—like dressing suggestively. When in doubt, shop. Cal won't be home until seven tonight and I can still waddle with the best of them. Go get cleaned up. Let's drive to Chattanooga and find you some wild-girl duds."

"I already have a dress for the reunion," Kate said, suddenly feeling cautious again. She couldn't imagine showing up at the gathering in some humiliating getup—wild or not.

"Oh, don't worry about the reunion. We have—" she counted off fingers "—one, two, three nights until then. Plenty of time to get you arrested...or something."

"Where am I going to wear these suggestive clothes?" Kate asked, dreading the answer.

"Why there're a couple of places where you could turn some heads. But it's too obvious to show up at your daddy's country club. I think you *have* to go to The Raven."

Kate looked at her cherub-faced best friend and wondered how she'd ever settled down and started a family. "You're evil, you know that, don't you?"

"Yeah. And I'm having more fun than I've had in years." Julie jumped then laughed as she ran a hand over her belly. "Even the baby is enjoying this."

"You better hope you have a boy because it would serve you right to end up with a wild girl."

"Shoot, I'll tell her like I told you. As long as you don't hurt anyone else or yourself, do like the army says—be all that you can be."

Kate couldn't argue with that logic.

"I'D LIKE TO SPEAK to Mr. Sutherland, please." Mitch leaned back in his office chair and waited for Terry Sutherland's secretary to put him on the line. He didn't know precisely what he intended to say but he felt he had to bring up the subject of Kate's unusual behavior with her father. He wanted to help if he could.

"Hey, Mitch. Sorry for the wait. I was in the middle

of a conference call." Terry Sutherland sounded all business.

"I can try back later if it's more convenient," Mitch offered.

Terry's famous "good ole boy" demeanor kicked in, all benevolent and helpful. "No. That's all right, son. The boys and I can continue that particular conference on the golf course tomorrow," Terry Sutherland said and then chuckled. "What can I do you for?"

"Well..." Now, with Kate's father on the phone, he had to think of a way to talk about Kate without feeling like he was betraying her. "I wanted to ask about Kate."

"Katie? What about her?"

"Well, she— uh— she's been acting different. She seems a little agitated." What he wanted to say was that she had mutated into a trouble-making hellion but that was a little strong for Kate's father to hear.

"Agitated? My Kate? Nah, she seems fine to me. If you mean that little stunt of taking Old Henry into Al's, don't worry about it. I paid Al for his trouble and he's forgotten the whole thing."

"How about the soda machine at the Shell station?"

There was a moment of silence before Terry said, "You got me there. What about the Shell station?"

So, Bob hadn't called on his boss to pay for Kate's trashing of the soda machine. Not surprising. Not too many folks in this town wanted to take on Terry Sutherland over his daughter.

"Should I give Bob a call?" Terry asked.

Deciding to let that particular dog lie, he changed directions. "No, that's not necessary. I took care of it. Mr. Sutherland, when did you see Kate last?"

Another few beats of silence passed before he answered. "Well, she was over at Carrie's yesterday. Carrie said she seemed just fine."

"So you haven't spoken to her yourself?"

"No, I had a full calendar this week. This reunion thing was last minute. Knew she was comin' into town, but we haven't gotten together. I'm sure I'll see her before she leaves."

Mitch felt a pang of sympathy for Kate. Her own father couldn't fit her into his schedule. The man was a tyrant and a fool. Then, the inner bad-boy Mitch had so painstakingly tamed woke up and smiled. He knew he shouldn't encourage the feeling but he couldn't help it. Kate brought out the hellion in him, it seemed. "Do you happen to know where she's staying?" Mitch asked, just for the hell of it.

"Why, I believe she's staying with that friend of hers, Janie or Julie. Don't know her last name though."

Mitch knew very well where Kate was staying, he'd driven her there two nights before. But he'd had enough of the man he'd only ever been able to take small doses of in the past. Might as well give Terry Sutherland something to think about, if he gave a damn, that is.

"I think I'll go by and see her if you don't mind.

You know I always had my eye on her in high school."

The silence on the other end of the phone was deafening. Then Terry seemed to find his fatherly feet.

"Yeah, that Kate's always been a good girl. Sailed through school, got a good job out there in California. She was never meant for Chapel, or any small town for that matter."

Mitch almost chuckled aloud. Kate's father didn't know it but the good girl luster was wearing thin. She'd declared herself a "wild girl" when she'd defiantly faced the chief of police wearing his handcuffs. And for just a moment, she'd no longer been shy little Kate from school and she'd almost convinced him she'd changed.

Never meant for a small town—the men *in a small town*. Mitch had a feeling her father was in for a big surprise—especially if he thought a muted warning to leave his daughter alone would be successful on someone like himself. Maybe he'd worked so hard to get respectable, people had forgotten that telling him no for no apparent reason only pushed him to get creative. Hell, maybe it was time for a little wildness, just to remind them.

"You know, I've always wanted to visit California again," Mitch said. "Haven't been there since I was stationed at Pendleton. I'd jump at the chance to go." Before Terry could respond, Mitch thought it better to get out while the gettin' was possible. "I'll tell Kate you said hello when I see her."

"You do that," Terry Sutherland said, but his benevolent tone had disappeared.

KATE ROLLED OVER and hugged her pillow protectively. The clock on the dresser said seven o'clock but she'd already been awake for almost an hour. She'd dreamed and dreamed until the last dream had woken her up. In it she'd been handcuffed, dressed in a black leather thong bikini and was being paraded through town by Mitch McKee. He'd half dragged, half led her right down Main Street to her father's office where the old man, after one horrified look, had turned his back.

It was all Julie's fault, Kate decided. After taking her shopping in several boutiques where Kate had tried on everything from leather to spandex to lace, she was now the proud owner of three wild-girl ensembles she was sure she'd never manage to wear in public. Julie had even urged her to try the clothes on and model them for her husband's opinion, but Kate declined. Not only was she shy, but dressing—or barely dressing—for someone else's husband seemed inappropriate—despite that Julie had been enthusiastic.

"Cal knows a wild girl when he sees one. He can tell you what to leave on and what to leave off. If you want more opinions, we can invite his poker buddies over."

At that point, Kate had the sneaking suspicion Mitch McKee might just be one of Cal's buddies. The thought of facing Mitch wearing little more than a few scraps of fantasy made her chest hurt. What if she didn't measure up to the wild girls he'd known? Even more reason to decline.

"When the time comes," Kate had said, "I'll decide what flavor of wild I can handle."

When the time comes. Kate thought of why she was doing all this. Her father. Today was Thursday and she'd be leaving on Sunday. She'd promised to take Julie to her doctor's appointment this afternoon but that left the morning and the evening to continue her plan.

The problem was, after facing Mitch's disapproval, she had no enthusiasm for the plan that just yesterday had seemed such a good idea—a desperate idea, but a good one nonetheless. Rather than make a fool of herself, she wished she could simply go to her father and talk. Tell him how she felt and straighten out any misunderstandings between them. She didn't want to interfere with his new family. She was happy he'd found a new life. But being completely excluded from that life was painful. He ought to be able to understand she simply wanted to be part of a family, the new and the old together.

Why did she have to run around town and humiliate herself for that to happen? Why couldn't she take the initiative and go to her father?

Throwing the covers back, Kate scrambled out of bed. If she could get their lack of communication cleared up this morning, there would be plenty of time to get to know her father and his second family again before she left. As she headed for the shower, she kicked aside the black four-inch spike heels she'd purchased for the wild girl. She wouldn't be needing those.

KATE STRAIGHTENED the jacket of her business suit and faced the carved oak door of her childhood home. Instinctively she reached for the doorknob. How many thousands of times had she swung on the knob or stood on tiptoes to tag the ornate door-knocker before Carrie? How many times had she opened the door and run through without question-ing whether she'd be welcome or not?

Kate released the knob and pressed the doorbell. After a few moments—long enough for Kate's ner-vousness to escalate—a maid Kate didn't recognize answered the door. She only opened it partway.

"Hi," Kate said. "I'm Kate Sutherland. I know it's early but I was hoping to see my father."

The maid looked her up and down. "Please wait here." Then to Kate's amazement, the woman closed the door.

Be calm, Kate chanted. *Just because the maid doesn't know you*— The door opened again and her father stood in the opening.

"Kate?"

Everything inside Kate relaxed and she smiled, "Hi, Daddy." Then she realized he was still standing in the doorway as if he didn't intend to invite her in either.

"I didn't expect—" His frown stretched into a smile. "Hello, Kate." He moved then, giving her space to step inside before placing a perfunctory kiss on her cheek. "What brings you out here?"

Kate swallowed her disappointment. She couldn't say, "I wanted to see you—" not yet, not in front of the maid who hovered in the background. "I need to talk to you about something," she managed.

Her father looked at his watch and the frown returned. "Well, I suppose I have a few minutes." He turned to the maid. "Ellen, call the club and tell them I'll be about fifteen minutes late for my tee time." Then he put out a hand in the direction Kate recognized as his office. "Let's go in here."

Walking through the hallway was like a waking dream. Kate remembered every square of the marble parquet, every ornate molding and doorway leading to the staircase. But the wallpaper and furniture had all been changed. The old South had given way to the new Southern living—familiar yet completely different.

Kate's father settled her into the big leather chair across the desk from his own with the gallantry of a stranger. As soon as he faced her, he clasped his hands and asked, "Now what did you want to talk about?"

The glimmer of hope she'd been nurturing that he'd actually be happy to see her faded. His expression made it clear he would give her time, but only so much and on his terms.

"Well, I thought—" In horror, Kate felt a lump rising in her throat. *I will not cry. I will not cry.*

"Is there a problem. Do you need some money?"

Kate found her voice. "No. I thought I should come out and see you while I'm in town." She waited for him to say he wanted to see her as well.

He smiled. "Well, I'm sure we could make some time to get together. Why don't you give Edith a call and she'll set something up?"

"I don't want to talk to your secretary, I want to talk to you."

"Okay, I'm here." He looked at his watch again. "I have another ten minutes before I have to leave."

Desperately, Kate tried to find a way to bring up family. His new family would be a good start. "How are Susan and the baby?"

To her amazement, her father went off into a soliloquy about fatherhood. How the baby was finally sleeping through the night and that he looked just like a Sutherland already. Then he said, "You know I wasn't around much when you girls were little. If I'd known how much I'd enjoy a baby in the house, I would have done this sooner."

Her realization of his distance from her had been driven like a dagger into her heart. Now his obvious disregard for her feelings face-to-face felt like a twist of that knife. Kate lost it.

"Do you have a cigarette?" the wild girl asked.

The enraptured smile of fatherhood was replaced by a frown. "I stopped smoking before Terrence Junior was born. This house is smoke-free." Her father seemed appalled and Kate felt a small measure of victory.

No way to salvage her initial plan of talking things

out. Kate went for sarcasm. Maybe Terrence Junior could stand a little competition. "Since you're enjoying fatherhood so much, are you planning to have more?"

Without giving it so much as a second's thought, Kate's father cut her to the quick.

"No, one heir is enough."

"I NEVER MEANT to let you go to The Raven alone," Julie said. She sat frowning as she watched Kate slither into a black leather miniskirt.

"I've done a lot of things on my own," Kate replied. But her thoughts were preoccupied by the tightness of the skirt. It barely covered her bottom and was so snug she couldn't imagine how she'd sit down.

"But The Raven...."

If she'd been uneasy in her other attempts at wildness, Kate felt positively unraveled by the woman looking back at her from the mirror. Sexy? She supposed the men she would encounter might enjoy a skin show. She'd never left the house wearing so little. And she *had* to leave the house tonight, to put a dent in her—and by proxy, her father's—reputation. She'd show him what family really meant. The good, the bad and the ugly.

Unable to allow Julie to scare her out of a grand entrance to the most notorious roadside bar on this side of the mountains, Kate hiked her hands up to rest on her leather-clad hips and faced her friend. "Don't try to talk me out of this now. It was your idea in the first place."

Julie's gaze ran over her from the black spiked pumps to her legs encased in shimmery stockings to the strapless, faux snakeskin bandeau. She swallowed. "You look like Heather Locklear on a heartbreaker road trip."

Unsure if that was good or bad, Kate turned to face the full-length mirror once more. Ignoring her growing performance anxiety, she said, "That's what we were going for, right?"

Julie didn't answer the question. She changed the subject, or perhaps elaborated on it. "I think Cal should go with you."

"You can't be serious," Kate met her friend's eyes in the mirror. "Surely Cal wouldn't take you to a place like that."

Julie crossed her arms over her protruding belly. "No, not in this condition, but he'll take you if I ask him."

A pure feeling of love ran through Kate. She moved over and took a seat next to Julie on the bed. "You know what?"

"What?" Julie asked.

Kate squeezed Julie's hand in her own. "You're the best thing I've ever found in this town—the best friend I could ever have. That includes my own sister." Kate hugged her. "But I won't allow you to 'loan' me your husband. Think of what people would say."

"I don't care what people say," Julie said with a sniff.

"Well, I do, on your behalf. Besides—" she rested a hand on Julie's belly "—you've got your own wild child to cause plenty of talk later. Might as well allow her to start with a clean slate—otherwise it takes all the fun out of it."

Thirty minutes later, as Kate's leather-clad bottom slid over and settled into the leather seat of the Mercedes, she began to have butterflies—*not misgivings.* She was determined to do this—to do something crazy—after her visit to her father. In her current state of mind, her greatest fear was that The Raven would be a disappointment. For years the place had been a pit stop for local hard-partyers and out-of-towners alike. A combination sports bar, pool hall and dance hall on the weekends, there was always something going on at The Raven. And a good bit of the goings-on were questionable.

Her second greatest fear was that she'd arrive at the wildest place in town and everyone would ignore her. She was sure many women dressed in miniskirts and wore too much makeup. What if, even in her most outrageous outfit, people found her as boring and safe as little Kate Sutherland had been in high school? What was that old saying? "Couldn't even get arrested walking naked down the interstate."

Kate blinked away that image. She wouldn't go near the interstate unless everything else failed. Following Julie's directions, she turned and drove through downtown Chapel. Not much to see at ten o'clock at night. The town was built on a central square with stores and restaurants on the outside of the square and city hall on the inside.

A row of three police cars were parked in the official spaces in front of the jail. Kate swallowed, feeling another thrum of nervousness. If she managed to complete her mission, she'd be locked up in one of the cells in an hour or so. She wondered, who would be the arresting officer? The nice deputy who'd give her the Breathalyzer? Or would it be Mitch McKee?

The wildness she'd been nurturing rose in intensity. She'd be a woman to be reckoned with tonight. She'd challenge every man in this town—including Mitch McKee if that's what it took. Kate was determined to be bad and to level her good reputation into a disreputable heap.

The light turned green and Kate moved toward her chosen destiny. She'd tried everything she knew to get her father to care about her as something other than an obligation. Tonight, she'd be someone completely different. It would either renew their relationship or sever it forever.

MITCH PROPPED his feet up on the coffee table and flipped through the channels again. Absolutely nothing on television. He'd been home for over an hour after picking up a late dinner at the local steak place. He'd been fed, had changed into his favorite "hundred-year-old" sweats and had a couch long enough for him to stretch out on. So why was he so restless?

Could it be because Kate Sutherland was back in

town and stirring things up? Stirring him up, anyhow—with her wildness, her "what the hell" attitude. The half-grown Katie of the past had needed his protection, and he'd known enough to keep his distance. But this grown woman with dyed red hair calling herself Kate needed something else. As soon as he figured out what that something was, he might just oblige her.

As far as he was concerned, the return of Kate Sutherland had so far been the most interesting thing to happen in Chapel for years. If you didn't count Cal winning the regional bass tournament, that is. Then again, Mitch might be the only one paying any attention. Too much attention, he concluded. Maybe tomorrow he'd call Sherry, go over to Chattanooga and make a night of it. He hadn't seen her in several weeks, but he knew if she had the night off, they would both feel better for it.

But that wouldn't take care of tonight. He flipped through a few more cable stations before the phone rang.

As he reached for the receiver, he felt a surge of adrenaline. Technically he was always on duty. Maybe something interesting *had* occurred in the small town of Chapel. Something that required the chief. "Hello?"

"Hey, Mitch," Cal Blake said.

Damn. No work. "Hey, buddy. What's goin' on?"

"Well, it's like this—" he started, then paused "—Julie and I—"

Mitch waited. He thought he could hear Julie's voice in the background.

"Julie and I have had a little, uh, disagreement. I thought I might go out for a beer and let her calm down. You want to meet me for a brew?"

Surprised by his friend's announcement, since as far as he remembered Cal and Julie rarely fought, Mitch couldn't help but ask, "You mean you're going to argue with a pregnant woman then leave her home alone?" Sounded dangerous to him—not for Julie, but for Cal. Seemed to Mitch that if you left a hormone-crazed wife alone too much she'd come up with something very unpleasant to greet Cal with when he returned home. Like a gun.

There was another pause, then Cal cleared his throat. "Well, it's like this, she's throwin' me out—for a few hours anyway. So, will you meet me over at The Raven?"

The prospect of a cold beer and a game of pool instead of surfing the tube tipped Mitch's pain and pleasure scale. It might be enough to placate his wild side. He gave in. "Yeah, I'll see you over there."

"Oh, and bring your gun," Cal said.

That brought Mitch up short. "What?"

"Ha, ha, ha," Cal said, his humor sounding totally insincere. "Just a joke."

5

CAL BLAKE, Mitch's sometime fishin' and poker-playing buddy was what the locals would call "a big old boy." Standing every inch of six foot five, Cal happened to be one of the few men Mitch had to literally look up to.

And when he'd looked at Cal tonight, he couldn't help but notice that ever since they'd walked through the door of The Raven, Cal had had his gaze on the door. Didn't seem to matter that tonight was amateur night in the other room for would-be strippers. Cal seemed nervous. And that made Mitch nervous.

"Are you worried Julie is gonna drive over and catch you here?" Mitch asked as he waited for Cal to take the next pool shot.

"No, she knows I'm here," Cal answered matter-of-factly before striking the ten ball. As the ball tumbled into the corner pocket, Cal's attention returned to the front door.

Mitch chalked his cue and waited for Cal's next shot. "I have it on good authority that this place isn't about to be raided."

Cal seemed oblivious to his joke. "You know..." Mitch prodded, expectantly, "because I'm the chief of police?" But his buddy wasn't listening.

Cal straightened from his pool-shooting stance, looked past Mitch and said, "Holy Mother of—" in such reverent awe Mitch had to turn and look as well.

A woman who looked a lot like Katie Sutherland stood just inside the front door. She appeared dazed for a moment by the dim light of the room and paused to let her eyes adjust.

Mitch's eyes had already adjusted and what he saw made him feel like he'd been whacked in the chest by the swing of a pool cue. It *was* Kate Sutherland. "Damn," he said, with feeling.

Kate's head came up as if she'd heard him. She gathered herself like a long-limbed cat, straightening her spine and moving forward, prowling more than walking. Mitch felt something low and dark stir inside him. He'd seen Kate's legs before and he'd seen her get worked up over a soda machine, but this woman, this Kate, was a stranger, a dangerous stranger to be reckoned with...or surrendered to. As a former marine, he'd never surrender. He might volunteer for a little hazardous duty, however. He was sure the gaze of every man in the vicinity followed those incredible legs covered by smoky-black stockings, and that great butt barely covered by black leather, as she crossed from the door to the bar. But he couldn't spare a glance for their reactions; he couldn't draw his gaze away from Kate.

"This is gonna be harder than I thought," Cal said in a dejected voice. He'd moved up next to Mitch to watch the Sutherland slither.

It took another minute for Cal's words to sink in.

Mitch turned his attention to his friend. "What are you talking about?" he asked.

Cal finally looked him in the eye. "I'm supposed to watch out for her," he confessed.

"So she knew the two of us would be here to play big brothers? Is that why she's dressed that way?"

"No." Cal nudged Mitch to turn back to their game. "The only one who knew is the one who sent me—Julie. And now you," Cal finished by hitting another ball but he missed the pocket.

"I'm just along for the ride?" Mitch asked.

"Well... Julie said it looks better if you and I are here together."

Mitch glanced toward Kate as the bartender placed what looked like a martini on the bar next to her. As far as he knew, no one who patronized The Raven drank martinis. He was amazed the bartender knew how to make one. He shook his head. Well, he'd wanted some excitement, and he'd wanted to see Kate Sutherland. His wishes had been granted. So why was he so sure that the evening would be a disaster? Maybe because of his gut instinct as a policeman...or, more likely, his pure bad-boy intuition. She was up to something. He could feel it radiating in the air around her. She wasn't armed, as far as he could tell, and she wasn't behind the wheel of a car. He studied her as well as he could from a distance.

Kate had turned sideways on the barstool to cross her amazing legs. Mitch couldn't help admiring their smooth length, downward from the patch of leather pretending to be a skirt to ankles he was sure he could circle with his hand. That's when he saw the ridiculously high heels of the shoes she wore. Her words from the first night he'd seen her echoed in his mind: *Be careful what you wish for.* A feeling of impending doom settled around him again. Maybe he *should* have brought his gun.

KATE'S EYES were beginning to adjust to the darkness, which was only brightened by several different colors of glaring neon light. She still couldn't clearly see the other patrons in the room, although she knew they were mostly men, about twenty or so—possibly more since she could now see a wide doorway leading to another room. Her heart was pounding so loud she was sure it could be heard over the jukebox. The faux snakeskin spandex covering her heart should have been undulating like a real snake. Doing her best to act as though she visited questionable bars alone dressed like a sex kitten all the time, she picked up her martini and took a serious gulp. As soon as she swallowed, she nearly choked to death. Resisting the coughing fit that would brand her as a rookie, she ended up with tears in her eyes. Blinking and taking deep breaths helped ease the shock of pure alcohol sliding down her unsophisticated throat.

The martini had one good effect, however, it began to warm her from the inside out. The bar felt cold, or maybe she was used to wearing more clothes than she currently had on. Whatever the case, there were goose bumps the size of jujubes on her arms and, without looking down, she knew her nipples had tightened under the thin stretchy cloth. Yearning for a little more warmth, she took a smaller sip of the martini before canvassing the room for someone to help her get arrested, or something.

That's when she saw Mitch McKee.

If she were the type of woman to swear she would have said, "Damn." Then she remembered that tonight she *was* the type of woman to swear and she did so, with gusto. "Damn!"

"Is there a problem?" The bartender asked.

Impressed by the immediate response to her change of personality, she gave him her best and brightest smile. Surely he wouldn't be able to tell it was a fake sex-kitten smile. "I think I need another martini," she said. "I just saw someone I don't like."

"I could have him thrown out if you want."

Wow, this really works, Kate thought, incredulous. *Damn.* She'd been missing out on an entire segment of life by being the good girl all the time. Resisting the urge to abuse her newfound power, she flicked one hand in dismissal. "Oh, don't worry. I don't think he'll bother me," she said with another smile. "If he does, I'll let you know."

As the bartender moved off to get her next drink, Kate looked back in Mitch's direction. He met her gaze across the smoke-filled room. He was standing, one hip against the pool table, one hand balancing a pool cue, utterly at ease in this disreputable place. Cocky. And for a moment she remembered him back in high school.

After class one afternoon, one of the senior football

players had picked a fight with a friend of Mitch's. When Mitch's friend had been bloodied and the fight should have ended, the football player wouldn't stop. So Mitch had waded in to make him stop.

Kate had watched the fight from a distance, her heart pounding wildly, too afraid to get closer than the sidewalk at the back of the school. But after it was over, and the football player had changed his mind about wanting to fight, Mitch had walked right by her as he and his friends left the school grounds. He'd taken off his shirt to fight and he was sweaty, covered with dirt and pieces of grass. His lip was bloody and another smear of blood, probably the football player's, decorated his chest like war paint.

Kate had been terrified and mortified and, as usual, unable to speak. Surrounded by three of four of his strutting friends, Mitch didn't speak to her either as he passed. He'd winked, perfectly at ease with his condition and her state of mind. She'd had to lean against the wall to steady her knees.

From across the room, ten or more years later, the new, tamer Mitch nodded to her without a smile, but something in the set of his jaw harkened back to the wild days. She nodded back before she caught herself. If he'd winked she would have probably screamed.

She didn't want to have any more trouble with Mitch. Of all the people to find in The Raven, why did *he* have to be here, the only man who could truly spoil her plans? When he turned to take his next shot, Kate's gaze automatically went to the way his jeans tightened across his butt as he leaned over the table. Now why hadn't she remembered what a nice butt he had? Then, realizing that she'd fallen a little too far into character, and before she got caught gawking, she forced her attention to the man at the other end of the table.

Cal Blake. Kate felt like killing Julie and hugging her at the same time. She'd sent her husband anyway—to make sure she didn't get in too much trouble. Well, she'd show them all that Kate Sutherland could be wild with the best of them. Including the all-time champion bad boy, Mitch McKee.

Just then the bartender returned with Kate's second martini. In deference to his delivery, she picked up the half-empty glass next to her and downed the contents. No coughing this time. She was getting better at this. As she handed the empty to the bartender he put down the full glass on the bar.

"So," he said, "are you here for the amateur contest?"

Feeling warmer and utterly magnanimous after a whole martini, and since the bartender had offered to have someone thrown out on her behalf, she again gave him her best smile. "The what?" she asked.

The bartender had a hopeful look in his eyes. "The amateur contest for strippers."

Kate had to swallow before she could speak. "Oh, that." She shrugged her already bare shoulders. "I might be. When does it take place?"

"At midnight," the bartender said before glancing at his glow-in-the dark watch. "It's quarter to eleven now." He waved to someone down the bar. "Gotta get back to work. I'm looking forward to seeing more of you." He grinned before tapping on the bar drumroll fashion. "That would make my night."

Left alone once more, Kate felt her smile slip. Kate Sutherland, Amateur Stripper. The title seemed to shimmer in her mind like a billboard. Was this the greatest opportunity to get her father's attention—hell, *everyone's* attention in Chapel, Tennessee—or had she completely wigged out? Her gaze drifted around the smoke-shrouded room. There were at least twenty men and maybe five women in this part of the bar. Since the far room seemed quiet, Kate assumed it to be empty. Could she actually take her clothes off in front of all these strangers?

She tried to picture her father's face when he heard the news. Whew. No help there. No one in their family had even contemplated something so outrageous as far as she knew. Her father might simply run her out of town along with everyone else.

At least then there would be no question about where she stood in the Sutherland bloodline. She'd be the naked one, on the left side of the family photo. Gawd.

She had another attack of nerves at the prospect and reached for the martini. She needed to think, she needed to calm down. Unfortunately, that's when Mitch decided to saunter across the room to the bar. No calming down with Mitch in the vicinity.

"Evenin'," he said, as though he wasn't surprised at all to see her there and dressed in leather.

Warmth from the alcohol again coursed through her but, unfortunately, instead of numbing, it only intensified her reaction to Mitch. Her nipples felt like marbles and her face and neck seemed to blossom with heat. When she didn't answer, he propped one foot on the bar rail and turned in her direction.

"Are you Kate Sutherland, or a figment of my imagination?" he asked.

"If I say I'm a figment, will that make you go away?" she answered, amazed her voice sounded so detached and challenging. It had to be the martini.

Mitch leisurely ran his gaze down to the heels of her shoes, then back up to her red lips before one side of his mouth hiked up in lazy, wicked smile. "I never imagined you quite like this, but I'm not complaining. And to answer the question, if you're *my* figment, then I'm staying put."

The smile unnerved her, as did his perusal. He'd never looked at her that way before. Well, maybe for a moment when she'd faced him after the soda machine debacle, but not with such intensity. The wild side of him he'd hidden from her when they'd been in high school suddenly overwhelmed her. Kate felt like her skin should be smoking.

"I think—" Kate began.

The bartender showed up. "What can I get ya, Chief?" he asked Mitch.

Mitch glanced at Kate's glass, recognized that it was full and made his order. "Two more drafts and a bourbon." Mitch waited for the bartender to leave before getting back to the subject. "You think what?"

Kate had recovered some of her resistance. She remembered that Mitch of all people seemed able to wreck her plans. "I think you should go back to your game. You can imagine just as well from across the room."

Mitch didn't move. "Are you waiting for someone?" He looked around the bar as if he expected to see her date.

Kate's mind raced as well as it could after one and a half martinis. If she told him she had a date, he would leave her alone. But then if she sat there for the entire evening without one, it would look like she'd been stood up. Her pride wouldn't allow Mitch to think that, not after he'd ignored her in school.

"I wanted to go out for an evening, and someone recommended this place. I decided to stop by and check it out." She'd spoken in her best businesslike tone to give credence to the words. Unfortunately, she'd slurred one of the words slightly and the urge to giggle about it surprised her. Above all else, she could tell Mitch wasn't buying it.

"How are you liking the evening so far?"

Kate glanced around the room just as the jukebox went silent. Rather than try to explain her motives to Mitch, she grabbed any plank in a storm. She carefully slid off the barstool and faced him before picking up her small, jeweled purse. "I like it much better with music." Concentrating on each step, she moved past him with a little wave and headed for the jukebox.

By the time Mitch made it back to Cal and the pool

table, two men were standing on either side of Kate ostensibly helping her pick out songs to play. They nearly fell over themselves digging quarters out of pockets and placing them in Kate's hands. At one point, she dropped a coin and a veritable scramble took place at her feet to find it.

Mitch realized he was gritting his teeth. He walked over to the ledge where his glass of beer remained half-full and his shot of bourbon, untouched. He picked up the shot glass and downed the contents, then chased it with the beer. It didn't help cool him off, but it did remind him to stop drinking. Above all else, he was the chief of police in this town; heavy drinking and getting angry were luxuries his reputation couldn't afford. Somebody had to keep a level head, no matter how much the effort cost him.

He lost the next two games of pool to Cal and had to fork over five bucks. Cal had relaxed after the initial arrival of his baby-sitting subject. He seemed happy that Kate was settled at the bar. Four men surrounded her now, all preening for her attention by buying her drinks.

Cal hitched his head toward Kate at the bar. "See? Everything's gonna be okay. She'll have her fun then I can follow her and make sure she gets home."

Mitch shook his head at his friend's naiveté. He picked up the rack and began placing the balls into it. "Cal? You ever watch those nature shows?"

Cal's eyes lit up. "You mean like bass fishing? Yeah, sure."

"No," Mitch continued as he threaded his fingers

among the pool balls to tighten them in the rack. "I mean the ones about the biology of animals, how they live, how they reproduce." Cal's frown caused Mitch to chuckle. "Well, without boring you with details, what usually happens is a bunch of male...let's say, sea lions gather around the females." He raised a hand toward Kate at the bar. "Sort of like those guys over there. And these males do all right until it's time for the female to choose one."

"Yeah, and...?" Cal leaned over the table and made the break.

As balls rolled around the table, Mitch said, "Well, then they begin to fight."

"Fight?" Cal repeated.

"Come on, Cal, you know what I'm talking about. How many fights have you seen that started over a woman?"

"Plenty back in high school," Cal admitted.

Mitch came around the table to take his shot. "Trust me. If there's one thing I've learned in the military and as a police officer, it's that a good many of us don't change much from who we were in high school." He looked over toward Kate again. "We just pick up new hobbies."

Over the next thirty minutes, Mitch managed to win one game out of three. The tables in The Raven's back room were filling up as men drifted in for the big contest at midnight. Some had brought their girl-friends and a couple had even brought their wives to compete for the two-hundred-and-fifty-dollar prize for the best striptease. Mitch was beginning to have a bad feeling about this.

As he'd done all evening long, he glanced to check on Kate. What he saw made his spine stiffen. One of the men, who had been paying way too much attention to Kate and who seemed to be the leading contender in the biology race, had bent and plucked Kate from her barstool and was carrying her across the room. Another man followed carrying their drinks. They were headed for the contest room and Mitch couldn't help himself. As they neared the pool tables, Mitch stepped in front of them.

For a moment, the man, who rivaled Cal for size, looked ready to order him out of the way. Then, he realized who he was facing.

"Hello, Chief," the man said.

Mitch nodded, then looked at Kate. "Are you having yourself a good time, Kate?" he asked. In the next instant, he thought he saw panic in her eyes. But she blinked, gazed up at her bearer and smiled what to Mitch looked like a fake smile. "I'm having a *wonderful* time, aren't I...?"

"Sandy," the man supplied.

Kate turned back to Mitch and licked her lips like she couldn't feel them anymore. Then she giggled. He'd never heard Kate giggle. He decided then and there that she was drunk. It hadn't occurred to him to count how many drinks she'd had. And with a six-pack of yahoos buying she could be in deep before she knew it.

"I think it might be time for you to head on home.

Cal can take you," Mitch said in his best authoritative voice.

But Kate was shaking her head. She giggled again. "I'm gonna do a script-ease," she said, fumbling with the word. She reached one slender hand out and ran her fingernail along the opening at the collar of Mitch's shirt. It was the first time she'd voluntarily touched him and the effect was electrifying.

"She's got a damn good chance of winning too," Sandy added. "Better get your bets down, Chief." With the still-smiling Kate in his arms, Sandy moved on toward the back room leaving Mitch silent and grim.

The protective side of Mitch knew there was no way on this side of hell he was going to stand by and watch Katie Sutherland do a striptease for a bar full of men. The wild side of him, on the other hand, conjured the sudden raw image of her sliding that leather skirt down, over the length of those legs until it was in a pool around the spike heels of those outrageous shoes. The desire that accompanied that image took his breath away. He could still feel her touch.

"What do we do now?" Cal asked. "Julie said to let her have fun but I don't know..." He scratched his head. "Maybe I should call Julie and ask what her idea of 'fun' is?"

Mitch didn't answer. He was back to figuring out why Kate was acting this way. He knew her...or he'd known her. She couldn't be this completely new person, not without cause. "I don't think she'll do it," Mitch said, finally.

"No? She sure looked ready to do it."

Mitch thought she had as well—fired by martinis and whatever was driving her behavior. But he had to hope she'd change her mind—for his own sake. There was no way he was going to allow this to go on. If she'd been sober, she could do whatever she wanted with his blessing.

"She'll chicken out," Mitch said again, hoping to convince himself along with Cal.

That's when the deejay in the back room cranked up the music. "Welcome to our weekly contest for lovely ladies who want to strut their stuff."

Mitch looked at Cal. Cal shrugged. They followed the bar patrons who were filing into the back room.

6

KATE WAS CLOSE to chickening out. She'd had cold feet the entire night, but three martinis had resolved the problem nicely. Now, looking around the smoke-filled room, crowded with eager male faces and smirking female ones, she felt what little wildness she'd artificially conjured begin to fade. She looked up at...whatever his name was, who'd gallantly carried her into the room and tried to gather her thoughts. Watching the man place bets in her favor with the men at the next table didn't make her feel any better. She needed someone to help calm her jitters.

Mitch.

Like a woman wearing spike heels and sinking into quicksand, she searched the room for the one friendly face she knew. Well, he hadn't looked too friendly a few minutes ago but that didn't count. He'd always been there in the background at school, looking out for her from a distance. Some deep down place inside her knew that no matter what occurred, Mitch McKee would help her, even if he only helped her as far as the county jail. Then she remembered Cal, Julie's husband, was here somewhere as well. She couldn't spot them, however. In the semidark room full of men it was hard to tell one from the other.

Another flutter of nervousness passed through her. Maybe the darkness was a blessing. The idea of stripping in front of Julie's husband was bad enough, but Mitch McKee...

"Baby," the man who had carried her leaned close and said, "you're gonna knock their socks off."

Knock their socks off. She wished that was the sum total of what she'd volunteered to remove in front of this rowdy audience. She glanced around the crowded room again. She'd wanted witnesses; it seemed as though half the male population of Chapel, Tennessee, was packed into The Raven elbow to beer bottle. Maybe Cal and Mitch had left...

A woman came over to the table and touched her arm. "Are you in the contest, sweetie?" she asked.

Kate did her best to focus on the woman's face. She looked to be in her forties, blond and busty, the kind of woman who might have been a real stripper sometime in the past.

Caught in her own diabolical plan of the present, Kate nodded as the man next to her said, "She sure as heck is."

"Come with me then."

Kate got to her feet and managed to walk a crooked line between the tables with an occasional nudge or outright touch from the men seated there. When she stumbled on the stairs leading to the backstage area, the woman steadied her.

"You sure you're all right?" she asked.

Kate could only nod. She couldn't remember being less all right in her life. But she wasn't Kate Sutherland tonight, she was someone else. Someone who wouldn't be floored by three martinis.

"We've got six girls. I'll put you last. Give you time to get ready."

Even a beginner like Kate recognized a warning that she needed to sober up when she heard one. Reality was doing its best to claim her. In a very few minutes, Kate was about to become an extremely amateur stripper. She'd never even danced naked in her own bedroom much less in front of another living soul. She hadn't seen the movie *Striptease* but her memory of the scenes in the trailer gave her some idea of what was required. She'd never look, or dance, like Demi Moore. So, her goal would be simple: to take off her clothes without falling down or freezing up in embarrassment.

As if they'd joined a team, the contestants were all given the same "locker room" speech. They could pick their own music from the list, they had to stay on the stage during the strip and they had to end with their panties still in place. Otherwise, they were warned, they could be arrested for indecent exposure.

Arrested for indecent exposure. The part of Kate that was furious with her father warmed to the idea. *The older sister of the heir to the Sutherland fortune, arrested for getting naked in front of an audience.* The rest of her rational mind was appalled. The warring emotions took Kate from a nervous giggle to the itch of unshed tears. She definitely needed to sober up. She'd assured Julie, and secretly herself, that she could do this—something wild enough to make her father choke on one of his monogrammed golf tees. Besides, crying would only ruin her makeup.

As the music began for the first stripper, Kate couldn't help herself and followed the other girls to the edge of the stage to watch. The woman in the spotlights couldn't have been more than twenty-two. She had a good body, built more like a gymnast than a dancer. She worked the stage rather than performed on it. As Kate watched the girl drop into the splits, she winced.

Kate had been barely able to get up the stairs. Her knees felt wobbly again. It was one thing to be wild and sexy—it was another to be drunk and inept. She'd worked to be the best at everything she'd set out to accomplish. And though stripping had never been one of her goals, she still hated the idea that she might get more sympathy than applause. She glanced at the men closest to the stage. They weren't smiling—only watching. Unsure of what that meant, Kate watched as well.

Then the girl on stage began to remove her strategically worn clothes and the room went wild. Obviously the audience hadn't come here for dancing or gymnastics. These men, the ultimate judges, had come to see skin.

Kate touched her fingers to her bare chest above the bandeau. *Skin. Legs and belly and breasts...* How had she ever thought she could do this? Kate glanced around as the girl on the stage finished her routine, searching for a way out. Unless she wanted to jump down from the elevated stage, it appeared she'd have to leave the way she'd come—by the stairs. She'd just turned the corner when she heard loud voices.

"Laura, I don't give a damn what your rules are! I want to see one of the girls."

Kate peeked around the corner. At the bottom of the stairs stood Mitch McKee, locked in verbal combat with the woman who seemed to be running the contest.

"You know we can't let any men bother the girls."

"I'm not bothering anybody. I just want to talk to her."

"No, Chief. We keep this contest legal. Even though you are the law, I can't give you any special privileges. Otherwise, we'd have to have a bouncer back here full-time."

Since there was no way to sneak out, Kate decided to leave with dignity and made her way carefully down the stairs. She'd simply ask Cal to take her home—if she could find him. When Mitch saw her, he seemed to bristle.

"Kate! You are *not* going to do this!"

She could have simply agreed with him because, after all, she'd just come to the same conclusion. But due to forces out of her control—either the martinis or the wildness she'd been cultivating—Kate bristled in response. "What do you mean?" she asked.

Mitch tried to push around Laura but she held her ground. She waved one of the bartenders over.

"I said you're leaving, right now," Mitch went on. "Cal will take you home. I won't allow you to do this. It's crazy!"

Kate's rebellion, which had been vacillating, abruptly took hold. "What do you mean you won't *allow* me? Are you speaking for yourself or for my father?"

"Chief!" Laura interrupted. "If you don't mind. I don't interfere with your business. Leave my girls alone."

"She isn't your girl, Laura," Mitch said. He gave Kate a "don't cross me" look. "This is Kate Sutherland, Terrence Sutherland's daughter."

Both Laura and the bartender she'd called as reinforcements turned to look at Kate. The bartender whistled under his breath. It sounded like a musical uh-oh.

"So?" Kate said, in a voice that reminded her of a nine-year-old in a losing battle. She hated that voice. Straightening her back, she looked at Laura.

"I intend to win this contest tonight. Please keep that man—" she pointed to the center of Mitch's chest "—away from me. He's not my father, he's not my husband and he's not my friend."

"Are you sure, honey?" Laura asked, apparently unsure of what to do now that she was dealing with Terrence Sutherland's daughter.

Kate had heard that tone since she'd been old enough to understand what it meant. *Terrence Sutherland's daughter.* Then she remembered what that distinction and a quarter would get her: a phone call to make an appointment to see the great man in person. "Don't worry, my father can't hold you responsible for what I do. I don't live at home and I'm over twenty-one."

The music for the next dancer blared through the hall. Mitch shouted to be heard. "Why don't you act your age, then?"

Kate conjured up her most wicked smile and aimed her next remark at the center of his disapproval. "I intend to," she taunted, then turned on her spiked heels and went back up the stairs.

Mitch was ready to commit murder, or worse.

"Chief, why don't you go get a beer and calm down. I don't think I've ever seen you so agitated," Laura said. She turned to the bartender. "Larry, you stand in this door. No one goes up that isn't wearing panties. I'm gonna go buy the chief a beer."

Mitch raised a hand to Laura. "I don't need a beer right now." He needed to get a handle on why Kate's stunt was making him so crazy. With a nod, he turned and walked back to where he'd left Cal. By the time he crossed the room, he was more under control.

"Did you talk to her?" Cal asked.

"Yeah, sorta," Mitch answered.

Cal took a pull on his beer and waited.

"She won't do it," Mitch said, sounding confident.

The woman on stage had done her preliminary dance to a pounding rock tune, now she began to remove her clothes. Peeling and twirling each piece, she waited until the men were hammering fists on the tables and shouting encouragement before obliging with the next.

Mitch watched in a detached sort of way. His mind was stuck on the image of Kate's defiant face. For the life of him, he couldn't figure out what she was up to. She could have any of the men in this room groveling at her feet without doing a public strip—himself included. He couldn't fail to notice, though, that no one but him seemed concerned by her lapse of mental health.

So maybe the problem was his and not hers. Why did he think he had to save her from herself, anyway? Maybe this wild woman was who she'd become after years away from home—although he doubted she could keep a high-profile corporate job in San Francisco pulling stunts like this. Who knew what went on in California?

There was just something not quite genuine about her actions. A sort of desperation that didn't ring true. His cop's instinct didn't buy Kate Sutherland, Wild Woman. Hell, he of all people should know one when he saw one.

He knew she'd been drinking. Earlier, when she'd been suspended in a man's arms giggling, his professional assessment would have been—waaay under the influence. But when she'd faced him on the stairs, she seemed sober enough to know what she was doing. Threatening to do, he amended.

The third dancer pranced through the curtains and inwardly Mitch relaxed somewhat. He'd been afraid Kate would march right on stage to spite him.

"She won't do it," Mitch said again.

Cal simply nodded.

"WHAT KIND of music do you want?" The deejay asked and handed Kate the list of songs.

Kate took the list but the paper wouldn't hold still because her hand was shaking. "You pick something," she said shoving the paper back at him.

"What do you like to dance to?"

Kate swallowed and admitted, "I'm not a good dancer."

The deejay nodded. "Something slow, then. Just groove with it."

Kate wanted to tell him she'd never "grooved" in her life, but he walked away and she was left with Laura. Laura was frowning.

"You don't have much to take off," she said, appraising Kate's wild-girl miniskirt and bandeau. "What do you have under the skirt?"

Obediently, Kate raised her skirt showing a garter belt over matching black panties. "Damn, girl," Laura said. "We may have a riot here tonight, yet." Becoming businesslike again, she motioned for Kate to pull her skirt down. "Okay, my advice, take the skirt off first, but don't hurry it. Then you can do the shoes, garter belt and stockings. I'd save the top for last. Got that?"

"I've never done this before," Kate blurted out. It was beginning to dawn on her that, although the contest said amateurs only, several of the girls obviously had some experience, or practiced a whole heck of a lot.

Laura leaned a little closer. "I'll tell you a secret most of these girls don't know. The best strippers pick out one man in the audience and play to him. Strip for him like he's your lover. You'll forget about being nervous. Trust me, that's the way to go."

THE FIFTH dancer had finished her routine three minutes before and already the audience was restless with a few men banging on tables, wanting Kate to appear. It seemed they were under some mistaken idea that The Raven had saved the best for last. They were destined for disappointment, Kate thought as she tried to calm her shaking nerves.

"Are you ready?" Laura asked.

Kate nodded before her knees got any weaker.

Laura signaled to the bartender, recently the guard of the stairs, to go ahead with the plan.

"SHE'S NOT gonna do it."

Mitch felt like he ought to pray but he wasn't sure for what. That she'd chicken out, he supposed since his lecture hadn't changed her mind. Although she'd shown quite a bit of backbone on the stairs earlier, he still expected her to revert back into the shy girl she'd been in high school, the one he'd kept his eye on for two years but never touched.

Then the curtains parted giving him heart palpitations but it was merely the bartender carrying a straight-backed chair. Okay, Mitch thought, maybe she's going to sit and talk or sing or—

Kate pushed through the curtains and the room went wild.

"Looks like she's gonna do it," Cal said over the uproar.

Mitch turned to Cal. "Go to the bar, dial 911 and get a couple of deputies over here. Tell 'em I said double time."

"But—" Cal started to disagree. The look on Mitch's face must have changed his mind. He put his beer down and pushed through the standing-room-only crowd for the door.

With Cal taken care of, Mitch looked at Kate. Big mistake. Her gaze locked with his and she gave him a sizzling secretive smile that went straight to his sex without passing go or collecting two hundred dollars.

What the hell was she doing?

She settled her behind in the chair and crossed her heart-stopping legs showing the fasteners of a garter belt. The stage light transformed her hair into a red-gold halo around her face. She looked like the Devil's own angel and the room fell completely silent. Then the music began.

In tough or emotional situations, Mitch's Irish always kicked in and this was no exception. Sister Agnes would have been proud. As Kate held him prisoner with her sultry gaze, he prayed for self-control. *Holy Mary, Mother of God, pray for us for we have sinned.*

He hadn't done a damned thing...yet. But with Kate pushing every one of his hard-earned control buttons, he felt reckless. Hot. Wild. Just what he expected she wanted him to feel.

Watching for his reaction, Kate uncrossed her legs and spread them wide enough for the audience to see her black panties under the skirt. Then, keeping time with the slow tempo of the music, she raised one leg and ran her hands from ankle to thigh. She did the same with the other and, without removing a stitch of clothing or taking her gaze from Mitch, she had every man in the room drooling in his beer.

Mitch had broken out in a sweat. Kate seemed intent on riling him up in more ways than one. Payback, he supposed, but at the moment he was too transfixed to fight it. The young girl he'd fantasized about was a full-grown temptress of a woman now, and as she slowly swayed to her feet, she kept him nailed with the sultry challenge in her eyes.

Mitch's breath caught in his chest.

Kate moved her hips in a slow circling invitation to him, running her hands from her hips to the apex of her thighs. As she teasingly pushed the skirt between her legs to form a temporary outline, envious eyes watched and sweating palms itched.

Keeping her movements in time with the music, Mitch watched Kate's hands disappear behind her. He was more mesmerized by her tongue, which had flicked out to wet lips red enough to stop traffic. Mitch's old instinct to protect the Kate he'd known in high school wavered. This new Kate—dancing seductively just for him, it seemed—set off something new and hot-blooded in Mitch. He hadn't been out of control since his wild days, and had thought that part of him had disappeared. But right now, with Kate challenging him, he was tempted to forget his hard-earned reputation and take what she offered. He wanted Kate, on her back and crying out his name in pleasure.

Truth be told, he didn't care who her father was.

When Kate began to slither out of her skirt, Mitch found himself moving forward toward the stage. The men around him seemed to have been struck dumb or turned to stone. There was very little audience participation. Until about three beats of music after the leather came to rest on her shoes. Then there was a rush of shouts, whistles and probably some begging going on.

The image of her with her skirt around her ankles was so close to the one he'd imagined earlier, Mitch had to blink away the feeling of déjà vu. When his gaze moved to the thong panties and the black garter belt gracing her slim hips, he realized he'd been much too conservative with his imagination. He'd never dreamed of Kate in such an outfit. If he had, he would have gotten her out of this place as soon as she'd stepped through the door, and kept her to himself.

Using the back of the chair for balance, she stepped out of the skirt before bending over and slipping off her shoes. Bending over was bad enough, but then she unfastened the clip holding up one of her stockings and Mitch's heart slipped into double time. He hoped he didn't have a heart attack before he could either get her off the stage, or, just get his hands on her.

Kate's hands were cold. The rest of her, however, was beginning to warm up nicely—not only from embarrassment, but from some other undefinable source between her and Mitch. She'd decided to follow Laura's advice and dance for him, mostly to taunt him for trying to control her. But something else had happened. She'd found when she looked at him, she couldn't pull her gaze away even if she'd wanted to.

And right now, she didn't want to. He'd looked dark and angry earlier. Now, as she slipped the stocking along her thigh, she felt her mouth curl into a smile. He was watching all right. She could feel his gaze like the slide of a hand on slick flesh. It made her blush, but it made some part of her, the center of her, heat with yearning. As if only *his* touch could soothe the ache.

She'd forgotten her nervousness. Vaguely the other men in the room registered occasionally. She'd hear a shout or a plea for more. But Kate's world consisted of the moody music, the wildfire sizzling under her skin...but mostly Mitch McKee.

Somehow all those yearnings of the young girl she'd been had settled and deepened. What she was experiencing now, the wildness of dancing and stripping for Mitch was stronger, and more reckless. Dangerous. She didn't have to find the right words, she could see it in his eyes. She'd let her body talk instead.

That's when she pushed the other stocking down

and off her toe. Mitch moved to the edge of the stage and some of the men in the audience started to notice what was happening between them.

With her music almost at an end, Kate knew it was time for the pièce de résistance—time to remove her bandeau. Using her connection to Mitch for courage, she ignored the yells of the men at the closest tables and kept her gaze on the one man in the room she suddenly wanted to strip for. Her own hands felt foreign as she ran them over her belly then plucked at the bottom hem of the stretchy top. Swallowing once for courage, she stared at Mitch and pulled the spandex upward to the howls of the audience.

That's when the fight started.

Suddenly Kate found herself in Mitch's arms having her clothes pushed at her. Someone had thrown a punch in the audience. Balanced over Mitch's shoulder as he carried her offstage, she thought she saw Cal Blake pick up one man by the scruff of the neck and throw a punch that propelled him over a crowded table of dance judges.

Cool night air caressed her barely covered body as Mitch pushed through the side exit and almost ran into two deputies. Mitch didn't slow down. He jerked his head toward the bar and ordered, "Get Cal Blake out of there before he gets killed. If anyone wants to argue about it, arrest them. We'll talk about it down at the jail."

Kate's embarrassment increased as Mitch gingerly set her down in the parking lot and handed her skirt and shoes to her.

"Here. Get dressed." The stockings and garter belt seemed to get tangled in his fingers. He pushed at them as if they were alive. "Put on what you can," he added.

Unable to look at him after spending her entire time on stage staring at him, Kate dutifully slipped on her shoes. When she straightened, Mitch clamped his hands on her upper arms.

"Kate, what in the world were you trying to do in there?"

Looking into his familiar frowning features kept her silent once more. But something had changed between them; she could feel it. For one instant, she mentally stepped back into the skin of the woman who'd enticed him with a striptease in front of a room full of men. She wanted to try that one more time, up close and personal. She gazed into his eyes, imagining that scenario. The effect was swift and hot.

With one exhaled breath of surrender, or maybe disbelief, Mitch swore under his breath. Then his mouth captured hers in a preemptive kiss that fulfilled all the dreams of what it would be like she could have conjured up. He wasn't gentle. He sucked at her lips, then bit the bottom one. He demanded her participation and she did her best to oblige. She clung to him out of need and shock. The need to recapture the feeling she'd felt when he'd devoured her with his eyes and the shock of how good it felt to touch and be touched by him. She'd never wanted any other man as much. As his hands slid over her back then around to the sides of her breasts, Kate arched into him, wanting more. Instead of giving her what she wanted, he pushed away from her enough to speak.

"If you ever try to take your clothes off in public for the men of Chapel, Tennessee, again, I'll handcuff you and take you back to San Francisco myself." He lowered his mouth to hers again.

Not given the opportunity to answer due to another kiss, Kate saved her comments for another day. She'd been wild, really wild, and she wanted to revel in it—with Mitch.

"Uh, excuse me, Chief?"

Hearing Les's voice as though from a distance, Mitch did his best to retreat mentally and physically from the pull of the woman in his arms. He managed it with great effort but continued to hold on to Kate with one arm to steady her.

When he turned to Les, he bristled again as Les's gaze ran down Kate, barely dressed in high heels, thong panties and her endangered top, before it returned to him. At least Les had the decency to blush so brilliantly that Mitch could see it even in the dim light of the parking lot.

"What is it?" Mitch asked as he bent and retrieved Kate's leather skirt from where it had fallen to the ground. Without words, he indicated for Kate to put it on.

"It's Cal Blake," Les said. "He's got a pretty good cut over his eye and the makings of a major shiner. I wanted to call him an ambulance but he won't have it. I think you should take a look."

"Cal's hurt?" Kate asked as she zipped up her skirt. "Where is he?"

"Oh no, you don't," Mitch said as she tried to walk past him. "You're not going back in there."

Kate pulled her back up straight and Mitch could see the indignant Sutherland strain showing. He decided to cut that off right away. "You're not going in there because you were the cause of the fight. If you go back, the fight will probably start all over again."

"Me?" she said in disbelief.

"Well, you and me," Mitch replied, relenting. "You decided to get them all riled up, then I stopped the show. That tends to make men fight, especially when money's been bet."

"Oh," Kate said.

He opened the back door of the patrol car. "You wait here. I'm not through with you."

Kate surprised him; she did as he asked. But before she got into the car, she touched his hand. "Please, tell Cal I'm sorry. I never meant for him to get hurt."

Fighting his own guilt for not being able to let the show go on, Mitch nodded. "I will. Now stay here, all right?"

It took more than forty-five minutes for Mitch to get the patrons of The Raven settled down and to extract Cal. When he finally returned to the patrol car where he'd left Kate, he half expected her to be gone. That would have been too easy, he decided as he walked toward her. Now he'd have to deal with her and if he expected her to explain her behavior, then he would probably have to explain his own. He wasn't sure he could. He opened the door for her.

"Come on, I'll take you home," he said.

She looked surprised. "You mean you aren't going to arrest me?"

"Do you want to be arrested?" Mitch demanded, more than ready to get to the bottom of her actions.

"Well...I thought..." She looked up at him in what appeared to be honest confusion and he put out a hand to help her from the car.

"Come on, we'll talk about it on the way back to town." Taking one of her arms to keep her steady, he walked her to his truck.

After getting her settled in his four-by-four he began the questioning. "Are you sober now?"

"Yes, I think so."

Mitch glanced sideways at her and was brutally reminded of the young girl he'd known in high school. She was slumped against the door, looking out the side window as though she'd lost everything and might find it in the dark. The clothes were different, the hair color, but not the look on her face. He'd seen that look before.

"Do you mind telling me what it is you want to accomplish by acting like you don't have good sense?" He had to work to keep his voice harsh and not think about the past. He needed answers and, by damned, he was going to get them.

As he watched, she straightened in her seat and searched for her purse. "I don't have any idea what you're talking about," she said in that infuriatingly stuck-up voice. "Do you have a cigarette?"

Mitch hit the brakes and pulled to the side of the road. "A cigarette? No. I quit five years ago." He turned to face her. "I want you to look me in the eye. If you're gonna lie, I want to make it as hard for you as possible." When she complied, he asked, "Are you a regular tobacco user, Ms. Sutherland?"

She raised her chin and stared at him. "That depends on what you mean by regular," she answered.

Mitch leaned closer. "Kate, do you smoke cigarettes?"

Okay, so she'd forgotten to smoke cigarettes during the evening, Kate remembered in disgust. There had been too many other things to deal with, like men and martinis and Mitch. She'd always been a terrible liar, so she'd given it up at an early age. Now that she'd taken up stripping, she thought she might be able to pull it off. But looking into Mitch's intense gaze took the air out of that fantasy.

"No, but I'm learning," she said finally as she opened her purse. When she withdrew the unopened pack she'd been carrying for two days, Mitch took it out of her hand and tossed it on the dash.

"Well, you're not learning in my truck."

Kate crossed her arms and feigned anger. The cigarettes had only been a ruse anyway. Being alone with Mitch after this evening—after the intimacies they'd shared—made Kate's artificial courage disappear altogether.

When Mitch started the truck moving again, he drove without speaking all the way into town, leaving Kate to wonder what he thought. She was beginning to think that silence was worse than the third degree when he passed by the turn that would have delivered her to Cal and Julie's house.

"Where are we going?" she asked unable to suffer the silence any longer.

"Why I'm taking you to jail, Ms. Sutherland. Isn't that what you wanted?"

_____ 7 _____

THE NIGHT SHIFT dispatcher looked up as the chief pushed through the front doors with Kate in tow. The air-conditioning raised goose bumps on the greater part of her exposed skin. But it was the look on the man's face that made her realize that other areas of her body had reacted to the temperature change. His gaze never left her chest.

"Evening, Chief," the man said. "Need any help?"

Mitch shook his head without an answer, but his expression must have spoken volumes because the man immediately forced his attention back down to the papers on the desk in front of him.

"Whe—where are you taking me? Don't I get a phone call?" Kate managed. Earlier in the evening, she had wanted this man's touch with a vengeance, now his big hand clamped on her arm felt like a stranger's.

He opened a door and ushered her through. "This is an interrogation room," he said and released her arm. "I want you to sit down. We are going to have a little talk."

"But I don't want to talk. I want to be arrested or go home." Kate knew she was teetering on the verge of tears and she couldn't stand the thought of humiliating herself in front of Mitch. Not after the way he'd looked at her...the way he'd kissed her.

"Kate, sit down," he said, a little more gently.

Gathering her dignity, even though she was half-dressed and close to tears, she set her purse—with one of her stockings caught in the strap and trailing from the side—on the scarred Formica table and took a seat.

"How do you like your coffee?" he asked.

Without thinking, Kate replied, "I don't usually drink coffee in the—" The look on Mitch's face stopped her. "Cream and sugar, please."

As Mitch went down the hall to the coffee room, he made a few decisions about Kate. He'd put her in the interrogation room instead of taking her to his office because he intended to get to the bottom of her actions of the past few days. If he actually had to put her under arrest, he would. She wasn't leaving this place until she explained to his satisfaction what had driven her to the stage of The Raven.

The uncomfortable notion that another man might be the problem slithered into his mind. Maybe some guy out in California had broken her heart and she thought she had to be different, act different to get his attention. If the guy showed up, Mitch would be happy to have a few quality moments with him on Kate's behalf. Hearts would not be what got broken.

Armed with hot coffee and steely determination, Mitch returned to the interrogation room. He expected defiance, threats of Sutherland retaliation and downright stubbornness. He could handle that. But when he opened the door, he found her in tears.

She futilely tried to wipe the evidence away as he set down the coffee cups. He handed her the napkins he'd brought.

"We don't keep tissues in the interrogation room. Usually our perps don't cry."

"Very funny," she said, but took the napkins.

He pulled out a chair and sat across from her. "So, are you ready to tell me about it?"

Kate took her time dabbing her eyes and her nose before responding. He could almost hear her mind whirring and calculating. "About what?" she asked as though the evening they'd just experienced had been a normal one in her life.

Mitch reached for his coffee cup. "I've got all night and plenty of coffee." He shrugged. "You're working on getting a reputation as a hellion in this town—tonight might have capped it. I just want to know why."

"What if I say it's none of your affair?" Kate said.

Mitch shook his head. *Too late, Katie.* He was in it, all the way now. "Tonight made it my affair."

Kate went very still as she faced him. "Why is that?"

"You're changing the subject. We'll talk about me another time. Right now, we're talking about you."

The first flicker of anger showed on her face. She pushed back the chair and walked to the far corner of the room. After a long, quiet moment staring at the green painted walls, she spoke, "I did what I wanted to do tonight. The last time I checked it's still a free country."

Mitch rose and followed her to the corner. Staring at the way her red hair just brushed the bare skin of her shoulders made him stop to gather his concentration before speaking. "I know what your rights are. What I'm trying to understand is what you hoped to gain from what you did this evening. What was the point?"

"It was fun," she said to the wall. She didn't sound happy though.

"Kate—" he touched her shoulder and turned her toward him "—you didn't look like you were having fun."

She gazed up at him then, her eyes sparkling with more unshed tears. "I did when I was dancing for you."

Her words hit him like a linebacker on third and short. Turns out she didn't need a good right hook to take him down.

"Don't—" he said, and swallowed. "Don't change the subject."

But her hands were sliding up his shirt front and her eyes were closing as she brought her mouth to his.

It would take a dead man to refuse her, and Mitch was very much alive as her sweet mouth opened for his tongue. It was slow and it was hot and it had to be right up there with one of the most erotic kisses he'd ever experienced. Where the devil did she learn to kiss like that? He knew she was changing the subject again, but the question raised by the heat escalating between them was the one subject he couldn't resist.

She kissed him as though she needed his mouth more than she needed air to breathe. And when she pressed the rest of her body against him—those amazing breasts he'd started a fight to keep hidden, and those hips spanned only by a flimsy scrap of black leather and lace—Mitch felt his erection swell and pulse. Damn, he wanted her. He'd wanted her since she was fifteen and he was seventeen and he'd seen her sitting by herself in the library at school pretending to study. Then she'd been off-limits; now she was half-naked in his arms. All he had to do was reach out and take...

One of his hands traveled the short distance from her back to her breast along the silky, stretchy material of her top. It was so easy to pluck up the edge and slide his hand underneath. A shudder ran through Kate's body at his touch, but instead of pulling back, she turned into his hand. A natural offer that he took, kneading her satiny skin and rolling her nipple to tautness.

Mitch knew there were a thousand reasons to stop and a hundred things he should say. He wanted to spend one more moment before doing the math, however. He deepened the kiss, taking her mouth in a manner that left no uncertainty as to how he'd take the rest of her when the time came. And after tonight, he had no doubt the time would come. He stroked her tongue with his own, tasting her and drawing her closer.

And then he stopped. First he had to know the why of tonight. Then they'd get to the when of them.

Holding them both steady, he straightened the line of Kate's top to a respectable level before running his hands along her arms and gently pushing her back.

Kate felt dazed and totally confused. It was the first time her body craved something her mind hadn't quite decided on. Since high school, anyway. The wild heat between her and Mitch wasn't her imagination, now. Nor was it the continuation of a high-school crush. It was real and elemental. And she wanted more.

Leaning into him, she tangled her fingers in his shirt and tried to draw him back.

"Kate?" he said into her ear. "We have to talk."

Completely lost in the smell of him, the rough, low sound of his voice, Kate pushed closer. "I don't want to talk. I want..." She took a deep breath for courage. "I want you to touch me, to—"

"Kate!" He shook her slightly and turned her body toward the empty room. He raised a hand and pointed out the video camera mounted in the corner, the red light as unblinking as an evil eye.

Kate sucked in a surprised breath, then felt a rush of warmth from her neck to the roots of her hair. It was one thing to do a public strip, quite another to have someone watch your most intimate moments with a man. She glanced at Mitch.

He seemed to expect her reaction. "Come on. Let's sit down." He took her arm and guided her back to the seat she'd occupied earlier.

With shaking hands, Kate picked up her cup of lukewarm coffee and took a sip to settle her nerves as Mitch reclaimed his seat across from her. When she set it down, he moved her cup aside and covered both her hands with his.

"I want to help, Kate. Please tell me what's going on with you."

He sounded so rational, so calm. She'd made a complete fool of herself, not only at The Raven but— she gave the camera a simmering glance— here with Mitch and she hadn't fazed him a bit. Instead of treating her like she deserved, he was still treating her like his little sister.

Except when he'd been kissing her, she noted. Nobody kissed like that to comfort or to be brotherly.

"Really, what does a girl have to do around here to get arrested, anyway?"

Mitch's calm demeanor disappeared. His gaze hardened and Kate felt an immediate stab of remorse. She preferred the helpful Mitch to the hardened policeman on duty.

His hands slid away. "Are you on medication or under a doctor's care?"

The implication of his question hurt. Kate had wanted people to think she was wild, not truly crazy. She did her best to look sane in the crazy situation she'd created. "No. I'm not on any medication."

Mitch shook his head. "Well, maybe you should be."

That hurt too.

"I'm just—" Kate stopped. Just what? A spoiled

child who wants her father's attention? That would be the basic truth, but it was more than that to her. "I'm just tired of everyone treating me like I'm little Katie Sutherland. I wanted to show everyone I've changed."

"Well, after tonight, no one is going to argue about that," Mitch said. He watched her for a long moment. "I still want to know why."

As she looked into his eyes, Kate had the ridiculous urge to cry again...this time, on his shoulder. How did he do it? Make her crazy for sex one moment then need his comfort the next? Maybe she *was* losing her mind.

When Kate didn't answer, Mitch went on. "I spoke to your father, he said you were doing fine. Nothing to worry about."

Nothing to worry about. A great feeling of futility settled over her. The entire, nerve-wracking, humiliating adventure of the evening, all for her father's benefit, and it was beneath his notice.

Kate gathered the defenses she'd perfected when dealing with her father. His daughter might not matter to him, but his good name that his new son would grow into mattered a great deal. She was sure of it. "He might worry if you put me in jail," she countered.

Mitch crossed his arms, not a comforting gesture. "I'm not gonna arrest you."

"But—"

"You didn't do anything illegal. Immoral, maybe. I'm not even convinced of that."

"But I took off my clothes in public and started a bar fight. Poor Cal—"

"For the record, I started the fight," Mitch said, sounding disgusted with himself. "And I owe Cal for taking the worst of it."

"I didn't see you hit anyone," Kate disagreed. "You were—" His hands had been on her, hiding her, almost dragging her off the stage. Her memory replayed the evening in fast forward. In those final moments of her strip, she'd been locked in a visual conversation with Mitch as she worked up the nerve to remove her top. He'd been close to the stage, she'd pulled the fabric up and then—

"I started the fight when I interrupted your dance," he admitted. "Several of your admirers thought it was a bit selfish of me and things got out of hand. If I hadn't had Cal at my back, I'd be the one with a shiner, and you'd have most likely won the contest."

It almost sounded like an apology and Kate was surprised. "Why did you stop it, then?"

He gave her a look that said she ought to know the answer. Finally, he leaned forward and rested his forearms on the desk. "Look Kate, I know I have no right to interfere with your life." He looked down at his hands. "Hell, I'm no angel. And neither of us are the same people we were in school. But—I don't know—I just have a feeling that if you'd talk to me, I could help. I don't believe you went off to San Francisco and learned to be a stripper." He waited for three heartbeats then asked, "Is this about a man?"

Unable to admit her real reason or argue about it

any longer, Kate told half the truth. "Yes." The man happened to be her father but she couldn't say that, not when Mitch technically worked for Terrence Sutherland.

The strange look on his face surprised her. He blew out a breath and ran one hand down his face before speaking. "I figured as much. You know, the best thing for a broken heart—"

"He didn't break my heart," Kate interrupted. "Not yet. I still think there's a chance we can work things out."

THE RIDE from the station to Julie and Cal's was nearly silent. Mitch seemed busy with his own thoughts and Kate was too tired to argue. She'd literally danced the tightrope tonight, on stage and with Mitch. She'd managed to mentally put some distance between them but, physically, she still felt the pull of his presence even after spending two hours alone with him.

They'd almost made love on the desk in the interrogation room and would have if he hadn't stopped. After her revelation of another man, the only indication of the fire which had exploded between them had been when Mitch, on the way out the doors to take her home, had made the policeman at the desk retrieve the videotape from the room and hand it over.

Evidence.

Evidence that her life was totally out of control. How could this have happened in a mere four days?

The popular adage *You Can't Go Home Again* should be a rule, not the title of a book. The way her visit to Chapel was going, she was afraid to consider what might happen at the reunion. The vague thought that her father might not be worth all the trouble surfaced. But Kate was too tired to sort it out.

When Mitch pulled up in front of the Blakes', the lights were still on. He got out and opened her door.

"You don't have to walk me in," she said, trying to look dignified in her bare feet and skimpy outfit. "I'm fine."

Mitch put his hands on his hips and stared at her for a moment. "I'm aware of that," he said. "I want to check on Cal if they're still awake."

"Oh." Then she remembered that her best friend's husband must have watched her strip. Gawd.

Julie met them at the door and ushered them both inside. Cal, who'd obviously been lying on the couch, sat up holding a raw hunk of beef to his eye.

"How are you doing, buddy?" Mitch asked.

Cal peeled off the steak and showed off his shiner. "I'm gonna tell them at work that Julie punched me."

Julie harrumphed. "No, you won't. You'll say, 'You should see the other guy.'"

Kate could see both Julie and Cal were taking this well, but she still felt awful. "Cal, I'm so sorry," she said, feeling lower by the moment.

Cal slapped the steak back on his eye and pointed to Mitch. "Don't be. It was his fault."

"Well, the two of you can argue about that," Julie

interrupted. She put an arm around Kate. "Are you all right?" she asked.

Tears welled up in Kate's eyes. "I'm fine. What are you doing awake at two o'clock in the morning worrying about me?"

Julie gazed at Kate for a moment, then past her to Mitch. Her eyes narrowed but she turned Kate back toward her bedroom. "I have trouble sleeping most nights anyhow. Come on. You look like you could use a nice, hot shower. We can talk tomorrow."

Truthfully, Kate was grateful for Julie's concern. She'd reached her stamina limit quite awhile ago. With one confused glance in Mitch's direction, she said, "Good night," then allowed Julie to lead her from the room.

8

"KATE?"

Reluctant to respond because it felt as though she'd only been asleep five minutes, Kate ignored the sound of her name. When she didn't answer right away, however, Julie shook her. "Kate? Wake up. Your father's secretary is on the phone."

Kate jumped, then immediately slumped back down. Moving made her head feel heavy and light at the same time, like a balloon half filled with water. Her equilibrium seemed to be out of kilter. She licked her lips and remembered why. Martinis, more than she'd ever had to drink in her life.

"Owww. I think I have a hangover." She slowly forced her eyes open and immediately regretted it. The world was beyond bright. According to her corneas, a supernova must have entered her bedroom sometime during the morning and then stuck around to torture her. Again she felt a pang of homesickness for the misty, gray mornings of San Francisco.

"Do you want me to tell her you'll call back?" Julie offered.

Kate moved then. "No. I—" It was rare enough for her father to reach out to her—even if the facilitator of that contact was Edith, his faithful secretary. "Tell her I'll be right there."

Julie left the room and Kate glanced at the clock. Seven o'clock. She sighed. Normally, she was an early riser like her father, but this morning...after last night...after taking off most of her clothes in front of a bar full of men...after doing her best in her own inept way to seduce Mitch McKee—

Mitch McKee.

She'd deal with Mitch another time. At the moment, she had more confidence in her ability to stand up to her father than to go another emotional round with Mitch.

Pushing to her feet, she raked her hair out of her eyes and headed for the bathroom. She didn't have the luxury to think about last night right now. Her head hurt too much to concentrate on more than one humiliation at a time. A glass of water to ease the croak in her voice, a wet washcloth to rub the sleep out of her eyes and some sweats to stay a little more covered than she had the night before and she'd be ready to face the phone and whatever message her father had sent.

It surprised her that he'd heard the news of her fall from grace so quickly. But then again, it shouldn't have. He was the leading citizen of Chapel and everyone in town would be itching to either talk to him, or about him.

Or about her.

Two minutes later, after her hasty toilette, she picked up the receiver of the phone.

"I'm sorry to keep you waiting," she said to Edith. Her voice sounded reasonably even, which surprised her.

"Good morning, Kate. I didn't realize I would wake you by calling."

"That's all right. I slept a little later than usual this morning." Kate made the mistake of glancing at Julie who was eavesdropping shamelessly. Julie made such a comical face along with a pregnant parody of a striptease, Kate almost burst out laughing. Instead, she cleared her throat. "What did you want to speak to me about?"

"Your father instructed me to invite you to play golf at the club with him and the mayor this morning. One of their regular foursome dropped out. Would you be available for a tee time of eight-thirty?"

Kate's heart took several hard beats. Her father was inviting her into his world. Even if a golf game wasn't Sunday dinner with the family, it would be a start. "Yes, of course. I'll be there."

"Good," Edith replied, businesslike. "He said if you need golf shoes or clubs to stop by the pro shop and use his account. He'll see you at the tee."

"Thank you."

Kate hung up the phone and stared at Julie. "My father has invited me to play golf."

"Is that a good thing?" Julie asked as she slid into the chair opposite Kate.

"I think so," Kate answered. The shock of the invitation was just wearing off, yet her hangover had disappeared. The invitation *had* to be a good sign. "He certainly wouldn't ask me to play golf with his friends if he intended to lecture me or disown me."

Julie reached to squeeze Kate's hand. "I'm so happy for you, Katie. Maybe he's finally come to his senses."

KATE PACED out of the pro shop wearing a pair of khaki shorts, a polo-type shirt, brand-new golf shoes, glove and carrying her new titanium driver. The rest of her new clubs would be delivered to the course courtesy of the shop. A good golf game was a little more complicated to come by in the San Francisco area. Consequently, she hadn't played in a while. But, she'd been a decent handicap for years since her father paid for both his daughters to learn, and learn well. She'd hoped to get in a little putting practice before tee time but decided not to cut it too close. As it was, Julie had had to drop her by The Raven to retrieve her car. She didn't want to be a laggard today and had no intentions of reverting to the wild girl.

Her headache had receded but remained a dull thud at the back of her skull. She'd choked down two cups of coffee and a piece of toast to calm her stomach, then dug out her darkest sunglasses to wear in the bright morning sun. Otherwise, she wouldn't be able to see down the fairways. Now she was as ready as she could be to play with the boys.

Her father waved to her as she approached the first tee. He was standing with the mayor, whom she recognized, and another man she'd never met.

"Glad you could make it, Kate," her father said. He

patted her shoulder in a fatherly way and Kate had to remind herself that she hadn't expected a hug. Terrence Sutherland turned to the other two men. "Mayor Dealey, you remember my youngest daughter, Kathleen?"

"Yes, of course," the mayor said and, smiling, extended his hand to Kate.

"Hello again." Kate smiled, feeling cordial until his hand gripped hers.

"My, you've certainly grown to be an attractive young woman," he went on, still gripping her hand.

Something about the way he was looking at her gave her the creeps. "Thank you," she said, responding to his compliment. She tried to take her hand back.

He brought his other hand into play so that hers was sandwiched between his. "I'm looking forward to seeing more of you while you're in town."

Alarm bells were clanging in Kate's mind, making her headache pound harder. Either the mayor had a natural tendency toward sleaziness or he had just sent her a message. For once in her life, she was happy she'd worn a golf glove for other reasons than her grip. Her father, without knowing it, salvaged the situation.

"And Kate, this is Jeremy Radsworth," he said. His interruption gave Kate the distraction she needed to reclaim her hand from the mayor's possession. "He's the British equivalent to our deputy director."

Shaking hands with Jeremy wasn't such a hardship. He looked to be about her own age or maybe a few years older. Impeccably dressed for a day at the country club, he could have stepped out of the pages of *Town and Country*. She decided to keep things formal for the time being to be safe. "Hello, Mr. Radsworth."

"Jeremy, please," he said as he took her hand briefly.

"Well, then—" her father rubbed his palms together briskly "—shall we hit the links?" He signaled for his caddy, then moved off toward the tee leaving Kate to choose between Jeremy Radsworth and Mayor Dealey for companionship.

Kate had never been called a fool.

"So, Jeremy, what part of England do you call home?"

BY NINE O'CLOCK, Mitch had already been in his office for two hours. He'd told himself he needed to come in early to prepare for his weekly policy meeting but he'd been lying. He hadn't slept worth a damn, for several reasons, the most obvious one being Kate. So instead of tossing around in his bed, he'd finally given up and come to work.

He'd been unprepared for the temptation lurking there.

Mitch glanced toward the videotape of him and Kate recorded in the interrogation room the night before. He'd locked it in his office to protect the contents from prying eyes, but who was going to protect them from him? He blew out a breath and shook his head. His memory of holding Kate, of kissing her and

PLAY
RUN FOR THE ROSES

...and you
can get

FREE BOOKS
and a
FREE GIFT!

Turn the page and let the race begin!

PLAY
RUN
FOR THE
ROSES

and get
THREE FREE GIFTS!
HOW TO PLAY:

1. With a coin, carefully scratch off the silver box at the right. Then check the claim chart to see what we have for you — **2 FREE BOOKS** and a **FREE GIFT**—**ALL YOURS FREE!**

2. Send back the card and you'll receive two brand-new Harlequin Temptation® novels. These books have a cover price of $3.99 each in the U.S. and $4.50 each in Canada, but they are yours to keep absolutely free.

3. There's no catch. You're under no obligation to buy anything. We charge nothing — ZERO — for your first shipment. And you don't have to make any minimum number of purchases — not even one!

4. The fact is, thousands of readers enjoy receiving books by mail from the Harlequin Reader Service®. They enjoy the convenience of home delivery...they like getting the best new novels at discount prices, BEFORE they're available in stores... and they love their *Heart to Heart* subscriber newsletter featuring author news, horoscopes, recipes, book reviews and much more!

5. We hope that after receiving your free books you'll want to remain a subscriber. But the choice is yours — to continue or cancel, any time at all! So why not take us up on our invitation, with no risk of any kind. You'll be glad you did!

This surprise mystery gift
Could be yours **FREE** –
When you play
RUN for the ROSES

Scratch
Here
See Claim Chart

YES! I have scratched off the silver box. Please send me the 2 FREE books and gift for which I qualify! I understand that I am under no obligation to purchase any books, as explained on the back and opposite page.

RUN for the ROSES	Claim Chart
👑 👑 👑	**2 FREE BOOKS AND A MYSTERY GIFT!**
👑 👑	**1 FREE BOOK!**
👑	**TRY AGAIN!**

NAME   (PLEASE PRINT CLEARLY)

ADDRESS

APT.#   CITY

STATE/PROV.   ZIP/POSTAL CODE

342 HDL C25R

142 HDL C25H
(H-T-OS-05/00)

Offer limited to one per household and not valid to current
Harlequin Temptation® subscribers. All orders subject to approval.

DETACH AND MAIL CARD TODAY!

The Harlequin Reader Service® — Here's how it works:

Accepting your 2 free books and gift places you under no obligation to buy anything. You may keep the books and gift and return the shipping statement marked "cancel." If you do not cancel, about a month later we'll send you 4 additional novels and bill you just $3.34 each in the U.S., or $3.80 each in Canada, plus 25¢ delivery per book and applicable taxes if any.*
That's the complete price and — compared to cover prices of $3.99 each in the U.S. and $4.50 each in Canada — it's quite a bargain! You may cancel at any time, but if you choose to continue, every month we'll send you 4 more books, which you may either purchase at the discount price or return to us and cancel your subscription.

*Terms and prices subject to change without notice. Sales tax applicable in N.Y. Canadian residents will be charged applicable provincial taxes and GST.

touching...had already kept him up, in more ways than one, all night. Sitting and watching a tape of it just might cause him to do something crazy—like driving over to the Blakes' and making several indecent proposals to Kate. He knew he couldn't do that, for many reasons, the main one being he wasn't sure he could take no for an answer.

But he had to do something.

He dialed the number and Julie answered the phone.

"Don't you ever sleep?" he asked. "That baby is gonna be delivered with little bags under its eyes."

"Mitch, what do you know about babies? Besides, I'd be grateful if this child would sleep through the night. We take naps, for your information."

"Speaking of naps, is our star dancer still asleep?"

"Well no, she's out at the country club. Her father invited her to play golf."

"Golf? I was hoping she'd have a hangover from hell and it would teach her a lesson. I'm in the mood to rub it in a little."

Julie laughed. "She looked slightly green around the hairline when she left. But nothing could keep her from seeing her father."

Mitch felt a pang of something he didn't like. Why should he care that she would drop everything and wade through high water and hell to see her father? She loved her father.

She wouldn't even pick up the phone to call you.

Mitch shut his eyes and rubbed them. He'd learned how to deal with frustration in the military—either redirect your energy, or run fifteen miles. Mitch had learned to redirect in a heartbeat. If he hadn't, if he'd been the old Mitch, he'd already be in his truck driving over to the country club. Welcome or not.

"Well, I hope she didn't wear her leather to the golf course. We might have to send the National Guard this time." He heard Julie chuckle and added, "Tell Cal I said hello."

Mitch hung up the phone and reached for the videotape. He'd intended to put it back in the bottom drawer of his desk, but instead he walked over and shoved it into the machine connected to a small television.

The image was in black and white, only moderately clear, but seeing Kate in his arms made Mitch's pulse pick up speed. The high angle only added to the slightly kinky thrill of being the voyeur. He watched as he kissed Kate thoroughly, saw her fingers digging into his back and he could almost taste her. When his video alter ego slid his hand under her top, his real fingers curled in response. She'd been so warm and soft and responsive. By the time the tape ended, he realized how close they'd been to making love right there on the table. Too close for the chief of police and Terrence Sutherland's daughter. How in the world had he managed to stop?

Thinking about it hurt in places that weren't open to negotiation. He pushed the eject button, removed the tape and replaced it in the bottom drawer. Then he went to the locker room to change clothes. So much for redirecting, it looked like he would have to run.

KATE HIT the first tee shot perfectly then sank the final putt at only two over par. Not bad for someone who hadn't golfed in months.

By the time the foursome reached the second tee, though, Kate knew several things. First, her father had no knowledge of what had gone on the night before at The Raven. She knew that to be the case because she'd noticed he was not very subtly trying to fix her up with Jeremy Radsworth, who had turned out to be a very nice, but also very proper, Englishman. Not someone who would date a wild girl.

The final thing she understood with certainty was that the mayor knew everything, and intended to use it to his advantage however he could. He took every opportunity to smile at her suggestively, to brush against her as he passed, and invariably he'd be standing behind her when she had to bend and place her ball.

When Kate's second tee shot hooked right into the rough, the mayor immediately offered to help find her ball. Kate had no intention of crashing around in the bushes with Mayor Dealey close behind her and said so in a more diplomatic way. Declining his offer didn't faze him, however, although it did cause Jeremy to volunteer as well. The three of them found it in record time. The next four shots put Kate well over par and had her father frowning.

As she hooked another tee shot, she turned to him. "I'm so sorry. I don't know what's the matter with me. I really do play better than this."

Her father patted her shoulder with a pained look. "Perhaps we need to have the pro give you a few brush-up lessons."

"I'd be happy to give you some pointers," the mayor said and Kate felt like rolling her eyes.

I'm sure you would.

As Kate teed up for the third hole, Mayor Dealey lumbered over to her and placed his large sweaty hand on her back. She could feel the clammy heat of his skin through the material of her shirt. Pretending he was giving her golf advice, he leaned close.

"I think we need to have a little talk about your... uh...extracurricular activities. I assure you, I will do everything in my power to fulfill any little fantasies you might have. I can be a very generous man." Looking smug and sagelike he patted her back, much like her father had, and said, "Now give it a whack straight down the center of the fairway." Then he spoke to her father and Jeremy, "I'm just going to stand over here and see if I can detect the problem with her swing."

Kate felt like swinging at him. Her memory of bashing the soda machine made her hands shake as she adjusted her grip. Her father and Jeremy were standing back giving her room to concentrate, whereas the mayor had taken up a position behind her, but a little in front of the tee this time, to perpetuate his ruse of being helpful.

Gritting her teeth, Kate took one practice swing. Her arms were still too tight. Heck, her whole body felt like wound wire. She stared down at the ball and told herself to swing like she was aiming at the mayor's head. A tiny twinge of satisfaction filled her as the club came down with a smooth swish.

She hit the ball harder than she'd ever hit it before. Unfortunately, it didn't quite reach the center of the fairway. It hooked dead left and hit Mayor Dealey right between the eyes.

Be careful what you wish for.

Kate was too shocked to move as he crumpled to the ground. Her father wasn't quite as stunned. He turned to his caddy. "Go back to the clubhouse and tell them to dial 911." Then he bent over the unconscious body of Chapel Hills' mayor.

"CHIEF?" Myra's voice came over the intercom. "Nine-one-one took a call about the mayor. Thought you'd want to know."

Mitch pushed the switch on the phone. "How bad and what's the location?"

"Don't know how bad but they sent the fire rescue out to the country club. Something happened on the golf course."

Golf course.

A weird premonition rolled over Mitch.

Kate.

By the time he got there, the EMT crew members were placing the mayor on a stretcher. Mitch glanced around at the curiosity seekers, the firemen and employees of the clubhouse before locating Kate standing next to her father. She looked like she might be in shock, still holding a golf club in her hand. Bill Henderson, one of his deputies, was talking to her and to Terry Sutherland. Mitch figured the mayor was in good hands so he headed for Kate.

Her expression brightened when she saw him. The look of unguarded need directed solely at him made his throat tight. By the time he reached her, however, she had reinforced her defenses.

He nodded to the group as he approached. "Terry? Bill?" He angled his head toward the mayor being carried off the course. "What happened out here?"

No one answered for a heartbeat and Mitch watched in amazement as Kate's eyes filled with tears.

"Well, it seems Miz Sutherland here hit the mayor with a hook," Deputy Bill said. "Or was it a slice?" he asked. "Anyway, knocked him out cold. He came around but they're taking him to the hospital to make sure he's okay."

"I didn't mean to hit him," Kate piped up before sniffing and looking away.

Mitch could tell her almighty Sutherland composure was hanging by a thread. He wanted to add some of his strength to her own but her father—

"It was an accident," Terry Sutherland said. "John was giving Kate some golf pointers and... Well, he shouldn't have been standing where he chose to stand. Kate's been having some problems with her swing..."

Mitch couldn't resist. "So she didn't hit him with the golf club?"

Kate's head swiveled toward him and at first he thought she might hit *him* with the club. But then the shadow of a smile played around her mouth.

"Of course not," Terry Sutherland went on. "Nobody, not even John, would be stupid enough to stand close enough to be hit with the club."

Everyone had missed the point except the one he'd intended it for in the first place.

"It looks like you folks can get on with your game," Deputy Henderson said. "They've cleared the scene." He glanced at Mitch for confirmation. "Guess we might as well clear out, too."

Mitch knew he couldn't intrude any more than he had. As the crowd had scattered, he'd realized that the well-dressed man standing close by must be with Kate and her father. A terrible possibility rose in his mind. Was this her heartbreaker from San Francisco? The man seemed to be the right age and, judging by the clothes he was wearing, he must be in the right tax bracket. If there were classic examples of the "haves" and "have-nots," Mitch knew this man was definitely the "have," and he himself would be the "have-not." The question of whether the man "had" Kate was too dangerous for his peace of mind. He decided it was time for him to get back to his own business.

"Be careful with that thing," he said with a wink at Kate. Without waiting for her reaction, he shook Terry Sutherland's hand. "Hope the day improves from here," he offered. As he walked away, he heard

Kate speaking to her father and the other man. When he glanced back, she was shaking the man's hand.

Something eased inside him. She wouldn't shake her lover's hand when she said goodbye. And she wouldn't leave the game if she'd wanted to get to know him better.

It was easy to find her gold Mercedes in the lot. Mitch leaned against the driver's door and waited.

9

A SHORT WHILE LATER, Kate entered the parking area, followed by a caddy carrying her father's gift—the new bag of golf clubs. Her head was pounding like a jackhammer and her heart felt like a broken piece of concrete. She'd finally gotten her opportunity to prove to her father she deserved a place in his life and she'd blown it. From the moment she'd opened her eyes in the morning until her last disastrous golf stroke and numerous apologies, the entire day had been a disaster.

Until she saw Mitch.

Tall and solid, leaning on her car with his arms crossed, he looked like a poster boy for the bad and the beautiful. He nodded as she approached but remained silent as Kate opened the trunk of her car and allowed the caddy to load the clubs inside. Tired of any subterfuge, she tossed her sunglasses in after them. She needed to confront the world as it was and what she'd made of it. As soon as the caddy was out of earshot, Kate covered her face with her hands.

"I didn't me-mean to do it," she confessed, her words half muffled by her shaking fingers. "I—" When her voice broke again, she decided against saying anything further.

Then Mitch's hands were on her, pulling her toward him, into his open arms. And she let him do it. She rested her forehead on his shoulder as his arms tightened around her, then he rubbed his palms up and down her back in a soothing manner.

"I don't care if you did mean to, as long as you didn't kill him." He chuckled into her hair. "I've never liked the mayor anyway. You probably saved him from me."

She knew he was trying to comfort her, but he didn't understand the magnitude of the disaster. After today, not only would her father never include her in his life, he'd get an even more sordid report of her activities at The Raven if the mayor wanted revenge. And Kate was positive someone like Mayor Dealey would want the maximum revenge. Then, without a doubt, the great Terrence Sutherland would disown her and be done with it.

Feeling drained, she relaxed slightly against the welcome support of Mitch's chest. It felt good, familiar. She couldn't remember the last time she'd simply been hugged or held. She could, however, remember the last time she'd been in Mitch's arms. He'd been kissing her, and she'd been enjoying it, more than she'd ever imagined she would.

With a sigh, she fought to regain her composure before she gave away all her secrets. "My life has turned into a soap opera," she mumbled into his shirt.

"I'd say it's closer to a demolition derby," he replied. In an apparent effort to ease the pointed humor of his words, he gave her another brief hug. "Come on, take a ride with me. You talk, I'll drive."

She wanted to say, "Can't we just stay like this for a while?" But she knew confessing that wish was a bad idea. For one thing, her father or one of his friends could see them together, and she'd had enough scandal for one week. Secondly, she didn't want Mitch to know how his simple offer of comfort made her want so much more from him.

"Where will we go?" she asked as she leaned back to look in his eyes.

His gaze searched her face, then his mouth twisted with a smile. "Someplace where you can fix your makeup."

Unable to locate her own sense of humor just yet, Kate used her elbow as a lever out of his arms. "Fine, let's go."

They'd been on the road several minutes before they had time to talk again. Kate managed to get her smeared mascara under control while Mitch contacted his office and instructed them to cancel the appointment he had for lunch and to transfer his calls to the mobile phone. Then she heard him explain that his absence could be noted as personal emergency leave.

Kate could only hear Mitch's half of the conversation and, after doing what she could about her face, her attention drifted off until she heard him ask, "When will he be released?"

He had to be referring to the mayor and Kate's stomach clenched, ready for more bad news.

Mitch glanced at her as he listened, then he smiled. He kept his voice stern as he answered, "No, Myra, Kate Sutherland did not hit the mayor with a golf club." He listened again. "I don't care what Sammy Jo said. I was there. Yes, I know you do. I'll tell her when I see her."

Mitch hung up the car phone but kept his eyes on the road. "The mayor is being released from the hospital. Looks like he'll have two black eyes. Myra said to tell you to hit him harder next time."

Kate wanted to laugh, she really did. Instead, her eyes filled with tears again. Well, she'd set out to gain a reputation...

Without warning, Mitch took a left turn on to a two-lane road which seemed to go straight up.

"Where are we going?" Kate managed.

"Larks Point."

Kate remembered Larks Point. Back in high school it had been the favored make-out location for a twenty-mile radius. It had a panoramic vista of the mountains, a spectacular view of the stars on a clear night and the area had remained relatively safe, unless a girl's virtue was at stake. Half the girls who'd grown up in Chapel had lost their virginity at Larks Point.

Since it was daytime, she had to figure Mitch's mind was on something besides her virtue—such as it was.

"Why Larks Point?" she asked.

Mitch gave her an evil grin. "What if I said, I

wanted to do what we never did in high school? Get naked under the stars and see what happens."

A flutter of arousal flickered to life low in her abdomen. As if his words could touch her there, as warm and as sure as his hand. Kate had to force her attention back to his question.

She decided to explain the obvious. "First, you may have noticed it's the middle of the day." She knew she should stop there, but the tiny spark of wildness Mitch had brought to life when she'd danced for him prodded her further. "What if I said you should have thought of that last night, when I was nearly naked, before you took me to jail for questioning?"

A moment of silence passed, her words rendering him momentarily speechless. Then he shook his head and seemed to change gears.

"Well, that's always been one of my failings, not dragging the bird in hand into the nearest bush. As for today, to answer your question, after your round of terminator golf, I think we need to hole up somewhere. My great, great grandaddy was a moonshiner and he had a favored expression that's been handed down. When the ax falls, don't wait to see whose neck is under it—head for the hills." He glanced over at her, "In this case, the ax would be golf club."

"You think this is funny, don't you?" she asked.

Mitch answered in a careful voice. "I didn't, at first, but I've gotten into the spirit of things."

When they reached the top of the winding incline, Mitch had to pay a bit more attention to his driving. The paved roadway gave way to gravel, and split in two directions. They took the left fork and soon they were on level ground, with the mountain on the left and a steep drop off to the right. Huge trees blocked the view of the valley between the neighboring mountains until they came to Larks Point.

A large patch of ground had been cleared and graveled to form a turnout. The only impediment between the gravel surface and thin air was a row of sturdy metal poles and a guardrail. The absence of trees provided a clear, one-hundred-and-eighty-degree vista of the surrounding mountains and valleys. A blue-gray haze floated over the distant peaks, giving visual voice to the name Blue Ridge Mountains.

Mitch pulled partway onto the turnout and stopped.

"Did you know that the city council paid to have that guardrail put up?" he said.

Grateful for a safe subject, Kate pulled herself together and responded. "Why? This is out of the city limits."

"They know what goes on up here and they figure, since they can't protect their sons and daughters from each other, the only thing they can protect them from is the consequence of accidentally hitting the gas instead of the brake, or knocking the car out of gear at an inopportune moment."

"How considerate of them," Kate said, feeling completely left out. She'd never been invited on a moonlit drive during high school, and unreasonably, at the moment she felt like that omission had somehow been Mitch's fault. If she'd paid less attention to him and more to the other boys her own age, in her own class, she might not have gone off to college a virgin. Or if Mitch had only asked...

"I imagine you used to come up here a lot back in high school," Kate said, then felt her face warm at the play on words.

Mitch gave a huff of laughter. "There were a lot more sexual fantasies going on in my brain than in my love life at that time. As a matter of fact, that's still the case."

Mitch had been her only fantasy. And being with him here and now seemed surreal. "Why did you bring me up here?" she asked, half hoping the fantasy would come true.

Putting the truck in gear, Mitch was all business again. "Actually, I didn't bring you here, to Larks Point. It's just on the way to the lake. Another ten minutes and I'll be able to offer you a cold soda or beer, if that's your choice. No people, no golf clubs and no interruptions."

The interruptions part of that sounded ominous but Kate was too tired and heartsick to worry. She leaned back in her seat and allowed Mitch to drive her where he wanted. Lately he seemed always to be taking her somewhere. She tried to picture how she would have felt if he'd put her in his car and swept her away when she'd been so crazy about him before, but it was too far in the past. Her only inkling came as a rush of that trembly feeling she used to get in her stomach whenever she saw him. Heck, even if he had stooped to taking advantage of her, he probably would have been vastly disappointed by her talent as a wild girl.

Barring her recent experience at The Raven, she wasn't much better at being wild now.

True to his word, in ten minutes, the lake suddenly shimmered through the trees. Five minutes later she was sitting in an Adirondack chair on a deck that connected to a small dock. The expanse of blue water bordered by evergreens, mountains and sky immediately raised the level of her mood from dismal to melancholy. The view was beautiful, almost perfect, and at that moment it only reminded her how imperfect her life had turned out to be. She didn't want to think about it. Taking a deep breath, she closed her eyes and waited for Mitch to return with her soda.

Mitch thought she'd fallen asleep. He stood over her, unwilling to startle her out of one restful moment. She looked tired, strained, with faint circles under her eyes. Part of that would be due to what had to be a righteous hangover, but her emotional reaction earlier seemed beyond a simple hangover.

But then again, what did he know about women, especially *this* woman? She'd baffled him from the first moment he set eyes on her, and truth be told, that was another good reason he'd kept his hands off her.

She scared him.

And that was a hell of a thing for a former delinquent, U.S. Marine and current chief of police to admit even to himself. All he knew was that he could feel her gaze on him, almost like a tangible touch.

He'd always known when she was in the room. He'd turn and she'd be—

Kate's eyes opened as if she'd been following his thoughts, waiting for a cue. Rather than show how much her timing had startled him, he stuck out a can of soda toward her.

"We didn't have any diet," he said.

"That's okay." She accepted the can.

Mitch moved past her and sat down in the chair next to hers. He stretched his legs out and crossed them at the ankles. This place had always calmed him and he hoped it would affect Kate the same way. He wanted to talk but he had to let her settle first.

"We get some great sunsets out here," he said, tipping his own can of soda in the direction they were facing. "That's west, and when the sun goes down, it paints the lake like fire."

"Who're we?" Kate said after taking a sip from her drink.

"Well, I bought this property when I was home on leave once." He smiled at the truth he was about to reveal. "I was never sure where I wanted to live or who I wanted to live with, but I knew where I wanted to fish. Anyway, Cal and I knocked together that little one-room cabin for a place to store our gear and in case of rain. He and I usually come up here to commune with the spirit of Granpappy Bass."

"Why are you still here in this Podunk town?" Kate asked. "You told me your job is less than exciting. You could go anywhere, do anything."

She certainly wasn't pulling any punches. Mitch

scrambled for a plausible answer. "I guess you mean besides the fishing?"

Kate turned her head and gave him a deadpan look. "Yes, besides the fishing."

Mitch thought for a moment about what was true and what was merely an excuse. "I put my life on hold when I came back here to look out for my mom. After she died, I felt that Chapel represented the only tie I had to the past and to my family so I decided to give it another chance. Sentimental, I guess."

"And how has that worked out for you?"

"You mean, besides the part about regularly wanting to pull my service revolver and shoot the knees off half the city council?" He shrugged. "I've already mentioned how I feel about the mayor."

"What about my father? What do you think of him?"

Mitch really didn't want to go there. But everything about Kate was connected to her family. "I think he's a good businessman. I already told you he's responsible for getting me hired as chief. But—"

"But?"

Mitch shifted in his chair, uneasy about getting between Kate and her father. "Honestly? I think he could use a few lessons in fatherhood, especially where you're concerned."

A yellow jacket buzzed past him and circled Kate's chair. Mitch watched as she waved it away. Then he saw her chin tremble and realized she was crying. "Ah, Kate. I'm sorry." He pulled his chair around until his right knee was touching her left. He picked up her hand and held it. "I didn't mean to hurt your feelings."

"It isn't you." She sniffed and wiped her cheeks. "It's him." She stared at Mitch's hand holding hers. "And me, I guess.

"You put your life on hold for your mother. Well I put mine in high gear for my father. As results go, I think you made the better choice. No matter how much I earn or achieve, my father simply acts as though he expected it."

"Is that why you haven't settled down and started a family?" Mitch couldn't believe he'd asked. But once it was out in the open, he realized he really wanted to know. "I mean, you're an attractive woman, there must have been men who—"

"There were men," Kate said. "I guess I was looking to please my father in that choice as well, searching for perfection instead of finding a man I couldn't walk away from." She pinned him with a retaliatory gaze. "Why haven't you gotten married and created the next generation of McKees?"

Relieved that her answer had contained nothing about broken hearts or vows of chastity, Mitch made a lighthearted stab at brightening the conversation with his answer. "Well, for one thing, you can be assured it had nothing to do with your father."

A tiny smile skittered across her mouth and Mitch felt like Granpappy Bass had decided to jump into his boat and save him the bait. He smiled in return.

"That's what this is all about, you know," she said. When he didn't reply, she added, "You asked why I was doing all these crazy things." She shrugged, looking a little embarrassed. "I was trying to get my father's attention."

"Do you mean to tell me that you hit the mayor in the head with a golf ball to impress your father?" Mitch asked, unable to believe his ears.

Kate pulled her hand out of his and playfully punched his knee. "No. I didn't mean to hit the mayor. It was just bad luck. Today of all days, I wanted to do everything right."

Mitch thought back and sifted through all her strange behavior during the week. "Okay. I can understand taking Old Henry to the diner—Al is a friend of your father's. And I can see the relationship between the Shell station your father owns and the soda machine you assaulted. I can almost go along with putting your Mercedes in a ditch. But you're gonna have to explain to me how doing a striptease at The Raven has anything to do with your daddy. What were you thinking?"

"The whole Raven thing turned out to be a mistake," Kate admitted readily. "But you have to see the logic. We—Julie and I—thought that if doing everything right all these years hadn't impressed my father, then maybe doing everything wrong would at least get him to react." She shook her head. "So far the only reaction I've gotten is from the mayor and you. She gave him a sidelong look. "I couldn't have done it if you hadn't been there."

That took the wind out of him. "What do you mean? I spent all my time trying to stop you."

"Yes, but when I got out on that stage, I was terrified. Then I found you in the audience, and danced for you."

Mitch was suffering through several different reactions to her words. One of them was pure sexual adrenaline. *She was dancing for me.* But the cautious part of his mind reexamined her words. He ran his free hand over his face and sighed.

"Please, don't tell me you were dancing for me but thinking about your father."

To his surprise, Kate laughed and squeezed his hand. "Trust me, in those moments when I was taking off my clothes and looking into your eyes, I had forgotten I even had a father. It was quite nice, actually."

Quite nice? She'd nearly gutted him with that shy but I'm-gonna-let-you-see-me, have-me, love-me look. "Yeah, I would say it was nice." He couldn't resist letting his gaze trace the line of her heartbreaking legs. Hell, she was just as sexy in khaki as she'd been in leather. "You nearly gave me a heart attack." He had to clear his throat and move on to other subjects.

"So what else have you got planned?" If she had some wilder idea than a striptease, he needed to know so he could be prepared. This time he'd need reinforcements.

Kate's good humor retreated into a slight frown. "I think it's time to give up. I'm out of ideas."

"Hell, Kate. Why don't you just drive over there and tell the old man what you think? What you want?"

"I tried it. I really did. Either I don't know how to express myself or he isn't listening. Besides—" she smiled again, slightly "—I'm beginning to think it's time I grew up. I'm a successful woman who's been living on her own for five years. What do I need a father for?"

Mitch, who would have given anything to have a father after his had walked away from the family, said the only honest answer he could muster. "I guess I've done all right without one. You can, too."

Just then there was a popping noise then a splash in the weeds at the edge to the lake. Mitch glanced toward the sound, then shook his head. "That's Grandpappy Bass reminding me again that I haven't caught him yet. The way things are going he might remain the famous 'one that got away.'"

Besides you, that is. Shaken by the stupid fear that Kate might be able to read his thoughts, Mitch blundered on. "How's your hangover?"

Kate squinted at him. "Better, I think. The headache I have now is from feeling like an idiot."

"I know an old Cherokee cure. Wanna try it?"

With a suspicious look, Kate answered slowly, "You're not gonna make me bait hooks or drink raw eggs are you?"

"No." He raised one hand like a witness being sworn in. "I promise. First we have to get you comfortable." He reached down and raised her foot before sliding her shoe off. In silence, he did the same with the other. He stood and offered a hand to her. "Now, stand up."

She did as he asked, looking puzzled but willing. "Hey, that's a nice watch," he said and slipped it off her arm. "Probably cost more than I make in a month."

Kate frowned at him then and he knew it was now or never. He deftly slipped the watch in his pocket, then bent and picked her up. She didn't fight him and, for a moment, he almost changed his mind. Maybe he should just carry her over to the tiny cabin, find a nice soft sleeping bag and put her down there. Tempting, *very* tempting.

Instead, he walked to the end of the dock and dropped her into the lake. She let out a yelp as she hit the water and went under. Before she came to the surface, Mitch had his shirt unbuttoned. He levered off his shoes as Kate pushed her wet hair out of her eyes.

The shock of the cold water brought a blast of pure fury along with it. Kate couldn't believe Mitch had thrown her in the lake. After her disastrous morning and all her confessions. *How dare he?* She'd trusted him, thought he'd actually been listening and cared about her problems. Well, as soon as she could get out, she would either throw him in or pick up a big stick and kill him with it. The recollection of the slightly used golf clubs in her car made her wish she'd driven him to the lake instead of the other way around.

"You *rat!*" she sputtered with feeling as she steadied herself on the sandy bottom. The water was chin deep which kept her from sinking further. Her blouse and shorts were no impediment to swimming, so drowning dramatically was out.

"How's your headache?" he asked as he shrugged off his shirt.

Kate swallowed. She'd forgotten all about her headache, as if the shock of the cool water had washed it away. But as she looked up at Mitch, bare-chested in the sunlight, the coolness of her skin began to heat.

"It's better," Kate confessed, spitting out water. "But isn't this cure a little drastic?"

Mitch took the wallet out of his back pocket, her watch and the money from his front pocket then stooped to place everything in one of his shoes.

He winked at her, which at close range seemed as intimate as a touch. "Not for an Indian," he said. Then he stood and dove off the end of the dock.

She felt his hands on her before she saw him. Startled, even though she knew no fish could have the strength to pull her under, she only had time to gulp a breath before the water closed over her head. Fighting seemed useless and as quickly as he'd taken her under, he dragged her to the top again.

"Why don't you act your age?" she demanded. Treading water was required now since he'd pulled her into deeper water. Indignant, she kicked her feet and glared into his face, the only part of him above water level.

He took in a mouthful of water and spit it in her direction, obviously more to impress than to hit. "I think that's the problem with most people, they grow up and forget how to play."

Kate acted as though she needed time to think it over. As he waited, she brought one hand up to push at her hair, but instead slapped the water and sent a drenching spray of water into his face. "I think you're right!" she said, adding insult to injury. Then she struck out toward shore. In two strokes, he had her ankle. In two pulls, he had dragged her back to him. In two heartbeats, she was trapped against his bare chest and gazing into his whiskey-colored eyes.

She tried to laugh and push away, but something in his gaze held her motionless. The lake water around them stilled as she watched droplets form at his hairline then roll down his face. His eyelashes were spiked and his lips were...close enough to make her want to lean into him, to lick the drops of lake water from the edges of his mouth.

"Does that mean you want to play?" he asked, his voice not much more than a low rumble.

Breathless, Kate could barely answer. "Maybe. What are the rules?"

He relaxed back into the water and gave her a slow-eyed look that should have steamed the water off her skin. "The only rule is you get to be seventeen again. No fancy cars or jobs, no striptease and no golf clubs. Just you and me, like we were in school, sneaking up here to the lake to be alone."

As his words sunk in, Kate's senses seemed to expand. Watching him as he drifted away from her a little, she could feel all kinds of sensations she hadn't noticed before. The languid brush of her wet clothes against her body, the warm breeze on her face that ruffled the water around her. Everything from the brilliance of the sunshine to the birds calling from the trees seemed to touch her personally. Then there was Mitch.

"Okay," she said, barely more than a whisper.

He stopped moving away from her then and Kate's heart pounded at a faster beat. She and Mitch McKee, after all those years of wishing.

Mitch moved toward Kate slowly. He didn't want to startle the dreamy expression from her face. He wished he knew or remembered more about how he'd felt at seventeen. He remembered anger, and he remembered lust. He remembered wanting to make sad little Katie Sutherland smile but not having one idea in hell about how to accomplish that.

But he'd made the promise to her, and he'd do his damnedest to keep it. He wouldn't have called what he did at seventeen making love. Today, however, he'd make love to Kate Sutherland, the way he'd wanted to so many years before.

He brushed his fingers up her arms and drew her close enough for her shirt to brush against the hair on his chest. For a long moment, he gazed into her eyes, checking for reluctance, hoping for heat. She raised her chin slightly, offering her mouth, but he wasn't ready to take it yet. One of the most excruciating and exciting things about sex as a teenager had to be the waiting. The yes, I will—no, I won't.

Kate had yes in her gaze, but Mitch wanted to

make them both suffer that tantalizing pain of having something just out of reach. Of straining and sweating, then being forced to wait, wanting more.

He brushed his cheek against hers, barely touching the corners of their mouths. On instinct, she turned her mouth toward his, searching for what she wanted. He kissed her cheek instead of her mouth and her hands pressed into his abs. A shudder of sensation ran downward, tightening his belly.

He worked his way across Kate's face, kissing her cheeks, her chin, the end of her nose. But at no time did he succumb to the lure of her mouth. She remained perfectly still after she realized her input was not required. But her hands, that was a different story. Whether she realized it or not, her hands were driving him crazy. She never moved them from the area of his belly or chest, but each time he kissed or nuzzled her face, her hands made up for what her mouth wanted to do. Sometimes grasping briefly with fingertips and sometimes digging in with fingernails, she made him want to stop thinking and just get on with it. Now there was a seventeen-year-old sentiment.

Finally, unable to wait any longer himself, Mitch began the gentle assault of her lips, as though she'd never been kissed and she needed to be taught, and coaxed and cherished.

The water lapped around his shoulders as he brushed his lips along hers, then investigated them with tiny licks and nudges. Soon she was breathing into his mouth and her hands were clutching his biceps. He framed her face with his fingers before giving her his tongue.

Slow. Ever so slowly, he kissed her, savoring the wet pliable feel of her lips, the slick roughness of her tongue, the sharpness of her teeth. He kissed her until he himself needed to stop or move on to another type of torture. Then he kissed her some more. When he finally ended the kiss, he had an erection that should have levitated him out of the lake. And Kate—Kate was trembling like he'd scared her half to death rather than kissed her completely to life.

"You okay?" he whispered into her ear.

"Mmm," she answered, as another shiver went through her.

"You cold?"

She wouldn't look at him. She brought her mouth close to his ear. "Are you kidding?"

Her words sounded almost normal but Mitch could tell she was somewhere else. Somewhere he'd taken her. Now it was time to move on to the next place.

"Come on," he said. He put an arm around her and started moving toward shore.

10

SHE STOOD in the doorway dripping water as he unrolled two sleeping bags and spread them on the floor of the small cabin. He'd already thrown open the windows to the lake breezes, pushed back tackle boxes and boat oars. Now he'd made their nest. It wasn't much for two adults used to comfortable beds, but for two seventeen-year-olds, it constituted heaven. With one last flick of the better-than-the-floor mattress, he stood and held out his hand to her.

Without hesitation, Kate walked into his arms. A shudder of anticipation traveled up his spine. He felt as though he'd waited half his life for her. Then he remembered, he had. As gently as he could, he set her back from him, then began to work the button on her shorts. He held her gaze as he slipped the zipper down and pushed them off her hips, then steadied her so she could step out of them. Her blouse came next.

"Lie down," he instructed. Still wearing her damp bra and panties, she did as he asked.

Looking down at her, sprawled out on the plaid liner of the sleeping bag with her red hair damp and her wide blue eyes sparkling with pure female fire,

Mitch realized he might not be able to get out of his wet jeans. Not without injury.

He also realized that if he'd seen her like this when he'd been seventeen, they both would have had different lives. No one would have ever kept him away from her. Not her father, not his mother, not the state police or the marines. No one.

With her watching him, looking like a living page from a Victoria's Secret catalog, he went to work on his jeans. He had to force the heavy, wet material over his bulging erection and when he stood there, free and as naked as he could get, he saw Kate take several deep breaths. If he were a betting man, he'd bet her heart was pounding like a rabbit.

He lowered himself and stretched out next to her, then put his hand on her chest, over her heart. The pounding under his palm made his own pulse accelerate.

"Are you scared?" he whispered, close to her ear.

"No," she answered, but he could tell it was a lie.

"Scared is good. It makes you hypersensitive." He lightly traced his fingers down her chest and along her belly. Her stomach clenched just as he thought it would and he smiled. He looked her in the eyes. "You know I won't hurt you, don't you?"

Kate ran her tongue over her lips and nodded. Then she turned toward him, drawing him to her. But with one hand, he easily pushed her back down.

"Don't help me, now." The surprise on her face changed to uncertainty. He was sure her heart had set off on its race again. He chuckled as he leaned over her. "I want to figure this out on my own."

Her mouth. He wanted to seduce her again like he had in the water. Kiss her until neither of them knew where they were or how long they'd been there.

Kate watched as Mitch's gaze zeroed in on her lips. She knew he was going to kiss her. As he lowered his head to do so, she felt the sharp tug of anticipation from her belly to her breasts.

She'd been kissed before, pecks good-night from nervous acquaintances, even passionate kisses from men wanting to make love to her. But Mitch... She licked her lips as his mouth descended. No one had ever kissed like Mitch. His kiss was deep and playful at the same time, sensual and branding. His kiss made something hidden within her quake.

As he took her to that warm, dark, scintillating place again, she fleetingly wondered how he would feel inside her. He seemed to sense her need to speed things up because, as her mind shifted into fast-forward, his warm hand skimmed up the cool skin of her belly and unfastened her bra.

As his palm smoothed and cupped her breast, he withdrew from the kiss. Staring down into her eyes, he whispered, "I want to look at you."

Kate had the sudden memory of doing her amateur strip at The Raven and looking into Mitch's eyes. At the time, she'd experienced the excitement, but in a vicarious way—as though it had been her body but someone else up there had been pulling the strings. Now, being exposed felt infinitely different, more exciting, and more excruciating. She wanted him to look at her; she just wasn't sure she could stand it.

When his mouth slanted into a slight smile, she knew he could guess what she wanted. He pushed back and propped himself on one elbow, leaving his other hand free to roam.

As he covered every inch of her sensitive skin with his warm hand, Kate had to squirm.

"So pretty," he said then plucked at her right nipple.

Suddenly feeling shy, she brought her hand up to hide her response. He brushed her hand away.

"Let me."

If words could be aphrodisiacs then those two, uttered with the unvarnished need she could hear in his voice, melted any resistance and recast it into cooperation. She wanted to touch him, to accelerate this exquisite torture, but again as she tried, he brushed off her efforts.

"Be still and let me do this," he ordered, beginning to sound exasperated.

Kate didn't want to exasperate him. She wanted to help, to participate—

In the middle of her thoughts, he'd lowered his mouth to her nipple and the wet heat scattered any left over strategies. Kate knew she'd never experienced anything so wonderful before this moment and she didn't want to spoil it by thinking.

Mitch felt Kate gasp in a breath as he sucked at her flesh. He would have smiled if his mouth hadn't been so busy. To say he was enjoying himself would be like saying the marines "liked" to fight—a poor relation to the truth.

He switched to her other nipple and lavished it with the attention he'd recently given her mouth. He wanted every part of her lit up like a Christmas tree, then he'd get down to the presents.

After he had dampened both nipples with his tongue, he blew lightly on them and watched as they puckered even tighter.

"You have beautiful breasts, Katie. And they like my touch."

Again, Kate tried to pull him closer, to return the favor, he figured. None of that, not yet. He laughed and pushed up to a kneeling position between her legs. "Let's see what else we have here." He took his time gazing at her face, the embarrassed pinkness of her neck and chest, those beautiful breasts. He remembered his absolute horror at the prospect of her baring those breasts in The Raven. Now he knew they were worth the fight.

Just for kicks, he leaned over and teased them again causing Kate to jump and arch her back upward. After pleasing himself by sucking until she moaned, he moved downward. Smooth belly, an innie belly button begging for his tongue. He was so lost in his exploration he forgot the past, the present, everything except the woman underneath him. Until he bumped his butt against the small refrigerator along the wall.

"Scoot up," he ordered, and helped Kate oblige. That put him face-to-face with the only piece of clothing Kate still wore. Her damp panties. Without warning, he pressed his face into the material, drawing in a deep satisfying breath. She smelled of expensive perfume, lake water and sex.

Kate had gone absolutely still beneath him. He nuzzled her through the thin material, breathing in more of her scent, then touched the center of the fragrant triangle with his tongue. Kate gasped and started to sit up. He used his hands to push her down again while he used his tongue to re-dampen the silk over the most sensitive parts it obscured. He was enjoying the hell out of this. Some part of his brain observed that perhaps grown-ups were too quick to shed their clothes. Leaving a few things on offered the opportunity of erotic torture.

With one finger, he pulled aside the elastic along the inside of her thigh. Then he licked the length of where the elastic had been. He did the same on the other side. All that remained to be licked was right down the center. Kate was trembling now, and trying to coax him closer to that goal. But Mitch had a different idea. He licked her through the panties again, making them wet with his tongue and with her excitement. Then instead of moving on, he pushed his mouth against her most sensitive nub and sucked, pulling underwear and skin into his mouth. She pulsed once against his tongue and he held fast sucking in harder using the underwear and his tongue for friction, then Kate's hands were in his hair, dragging him closer. She climaxed with a keening moan that would make any man howl at the moon. Mitch couldn't howl, he was too damned busy. He stayed with her until she'd collapsed back onto the sleeping bag. He felt a little guilty for keeping the ultimate touch out of her reach. So before he left the area, he pulled her panties aside and kissed the bare skin beneath, touching lightly with his tongue. Kate's legs twitched and she shivered slightly. He replaced her panties and stretched out beside her.

She had her eyes closed and looked as though she'd fallen out of the sky.

He kissed her cheek and her hair. "Are you okay?"

Kate felt like she'd been dragged up Lookout Mountain and then thrown off—into pure ecstasy. Nothing she'd ever done had been better. She opened her eyes and tried to smile, but her whole body seemed to be in a drunken sexual stupor.

"That was incredible," she managed. "Thank you."

The corners of his mouth kicked up. "You're welcome."

Staring into his amused and confident features, Kate suddenly realized all they'd lost by not touching each other years before. A sadness settled in around her heart. Mitch McKee—the reality had turned out to be much more exciting than the fantasy.

Kate brought her palm up and placed it on his cheek. "It's a good thing I didn't know you could do that when you were seventeen," she teased.

"Hell. I didn't know how to do much of anything then." His smile widened, making Kate's heart pound again. In that millisecond, she realized she could love Mitch McKee. Not like she'd loved him in high school, but the real grown-up kind of love. The playful side of him had cinched it.

"I know a few other things now though," he said and slid his hand down her belly once more.

She stopped him at her waist. "Oh no, you don't. It's my turn." She sat up and indicated for him to lie down where she'd been.

He hesitated slightly, then did as she asked.

When he was settled, Kate made a show of peeling down her panties and kicking them off. Then, in her best imitation of a long sleek cat, she stretched out on top of him. It took her a moment to get comfortable because his erection was poking her in the belly. But, after squirming until Mitch grabbed her butt to keep her still, she gazed down in his intoxicating whiskey eyes.

"Do you know what I'm going to do?" she asked, formulating her own brand of torture.

He stared at her before saying in a heartfelt tone, "Honey, *anything* you do is gonna make me crazy."

Kate felt her wild side blossoming inside her. Mitch McKee wasn't leaving this place without begging. "Count on it," she agreed.

Before she could advance further, however, Mitch went serious on her. "We have to talk though," he said. When she didn't interrupt, he went on. "I've been a careful man. I use condoms and I give blood every once in a while so I know I don't have anything that would hurt you. But—" he grimaced "—I don't have any condoms in the truck. I don't carry them in my wallet like I did in high school. And up here at the lake, I usually only dip one kind of line."

Kate kissed his mouth lightly. "I trust you, Mitch. You don't have to worry, I've been safe as well."

"Are you taking birth control?" he asked.

Kate started to tell the truth. She wasn't. Why would she be when she wasn't in any kind of steady relationship? But when she moved, she could still feel the tautness and the heat of him beneath her. And she remembered how it felt to be thrown off the mountain. She wanted to feel that way again, with Mitch inside her. They would fly together. One time couldn't possibly hurt.

"I, uh—"

"If you're not, there are other things we can do, you know."

Kate's conscience was out just in time. "I'm not, but—"

Mitch's hands pressed into her backside, grinding her into him. He groaned. "I could come just like this," he confessed in a thick voice.

"No!" Kate arched out of his grasp and kneeled between his knees much like he'd done to her. She hadn't had her turn at torture yet. Without pausing for discussion, she ran her palms up his thighs then took him in her hands.

"You're so hot," she said but she wasn't sure Mitch could hear her. His eyes were shut, his head thrown back. She squeezed and pulled and felt him pulse in her hand. Then she leaned down to kiss him there. The kiss became a laving with her tongue. She could hear him making sounds, but he seemed very far away. She was fascinated by the velvety softness and heat of him.

Suddenly Mitch pulled her head away. He sat up, dragging her to him, forehead to forehead.

"You've got to wait a minute or two," he sounded like he'd run all the way up the steep road from town. Breathless.

Kate gave him a moment, then she pushed against his shoulders to make him lie down again. He did, but he was watching her this time. She pushed his legs together then sat on his hips, his sex intimately pressed against hers.

"Kate?" he said, unsure of what she intended.

She moved then, the friction and natural lubrication between them facilitating the motion. Mitch sighed and relaxed letting her take control once more. But soon he was helping, pulling her down, pressing his hips upward.

When she'd started this, her only thought had been to give him the same sweet torture he'd given her, but now as she moved she felt her own body coil and heat. Creating her own torture. She was so close. She wanted, she needed Mitch inside her.

For better or worse, she *had* to have Mitch inside her. In one smooth arching of her back and shift of her hips, the wild side or her accomplished her goal. She drew in a deep breath and shuddered as his hot smoothness slid into her. Nothing in her memory had ever felt more right.

As her body closed around him, Mitch made a

sound she wouldn't have been able to describe except as her name mixed with pain. In a brief battle of wills, he made one move to dislodge her but she held tight.

Then he was driving into her. Gone were the teasing touches and playful kisses. His hands were rough as he grasped her hips, taking every centimeter of what she offered. They both reached the pinnacle within the same two strokes. With a cry of total completion, Kate collapsed onto Mitch. His body shuddered, but his arm circled her back to hold them steady. Kate listened to the thunder of his heartbeat a full minute before he spoke.

"Damn, Kate." His voice was a low huff of air in her ear.

"I'll second that," she answered. The hair on his chest tickled her nose so she tugged at it.

"Ow." Both his arms tightened around her causing Kate's heart to expand. She'd never experienced anything like what had just happened between them. She wanted him to say the same thing, but wouldn't ask. She'd rather cling to the fantasy, that she was lying in the arms of the man she loved. The man who loved her. That was the kind of truth lovemaking was supposed to reinforce.

Suddenly he seemed to gain his foothold on reality because in the next heartbeat he rolled, pulling free of their intimate contact and pinning her beneath him.

"That was fairly incredible," he said before bending down to kiss her nose. Then, in contrast to his light words, he kissed her deeply and slowly until she felt like every thought had been drained out of her brain.

He looked down at her with serious eyes. "We're not doing that anymore without protection. You got that?"

Kate nodded, undeterred. *Doing it anymore.* That implied they would be together again, like this. Nothing could mar the happiness his promise gave her. Being the efficient business person that she was, Kate decided to close the deal.

"I'll be checking into a room at the resort this afternoon for the reunion. Want to be my roommate?"

Mitch had such a surprised, comical look on his face, Kate laughed. In that moment, she felt totally free to be whoever she chose, to ask for whatever she wanted. She wanted Mitch McKee.

"Damn, Kate, we haven't even gotten dressed yet and you're already planning the next time." He didn't really sound upset by her declaration, so she let her wild side fly.

She slid one bare leg over his hips and pulled him close again. Remembering how he'd felt inside her, she offered him a look that showed just how hot he made her feel. "I liked it," she said, then licked her lips. "I want more."

Mitch looked as though he'd lost the power of speech, so he did what Kate wanted him to do anyway. He kissed her, like a hungry man at a banquet. Then he said, "You'll get as much as you can handle, Katie."

should they meet in the mall parking lot...

11

TWO HOURS LATER, Kate checked the temperature of the water in the shower at Julie's before stepping under the steaming stream. It felt like heaven. Every inch of her skin seemed supersensitive, as though Mitch's touch and lovemaking had somehow awoken her from a long sleep. Maybe this was how Sleeping Beauty felt. Kate smiled into the cascading water that rushed down her face. Get a grip. Her little girl days of believing in princes were long past. She'd put them away around the time her mother had died. She'd had to grow up overnight. It was a little late now to hope for a happy ending.

But today had been an eye-opening experience for her to say the least. She'd thought that after the disastrous beginning of her day nothing could salvage her optimism.

But that was before Mitch McKee.

She hadn't even flinched when she'd had to face her father again. Kate squeezed some shampoo into her palm and began lathering her hair. Her hair had still been wet and her clothes unacceptably wrinkled when Mitch had driven her back from the lake to the clubhouse so she could pick up her car. And who should they meet in the parking lot but her father and the perfect English suitor he'd chosen for her.

Kate's hands stilled as she suddenly realized that not only had her father planned to get her married off if she chose Jeremy, he'd also had the perfect way get her out of his life. It would be difficult for her to intrude on his new family if she moved to England.

Pushing that familiar pain aside, Kate decided she was glad her father had caught her with Mitch. She hoped it had been obvious what she'd been doing, but she couldn't depend on that. Mitch had been businesslike in his goodbyes, even when she herself had lightly kissed him on the mouth.

Still trying to save her reputation.

Well, it was too late for redemption now and Kate found she cared even less about what people thought of her than before. Even her father's machinations didn't have the edge they'd had yesterday.

Somehow Mitch had changed everything. Or, she'd changed with Mitch's tutelage. The memory of his hands running over her sent a shiver of afterburn under her skin. Holding Mitch's image in her mind, Kate closed her eyes and slid soapy palms over her breasts and immediately her nipples peaked. She wanted more. Mitch—

After three loud bangs on the door, Julie's voice echoed through the wood. "Are you almost done in there? You promised to tell me what happened today."

All erotic thoughts scattered like water droplets. There would be time for *more* later, when Mitch came to her room at the resort as he'd promised. A slow smile shifted across her mouth. Julie was not going to believe what the wild girl had done.

"I'll be out in a few minutes. Don't worry, you'll be the first to know."

"FIRST THINGS FIRST," Kate said as she made herself comfortable on Julie's couch. She'd had her shower and dried her hair, now she was ready to talk.

Over the next fifteen minutes, Kate gave Julie the high points of her ill-fated golf game, her father's inept matchmaking attempt and the mayor's sleazy behavior. When she reached the point when she'd hit the mayor with the golf ball, Julie covered her mouth with her hand. For one moment, she seemed horrified, then she burst out laughing.

"Oh, my God. You didn't!"

"I did," Kate confessed. "I didn't mean to, but he deserved it." As Julie held her stomach and laughed herself to tears, Kate added, "I hear he has two black eyes."

Julie went off into another spasm of giggling and Kate got up to get her a tissue to wipe away her tears.

"Stop! Don't tell me anymore or I'll end up having this baby here and now," Julie said, gasping for air and wiping her eyes. "What did your father say?" she choked out.

"Not much. He did tell the policeman that I'd been having some trouble with my swing."

Julie stared at her, then burst out laughing again. "Some trouble, huh?"

"At least I didn't hit him with my club. That would have landed me in jail."

Julie took a deep breath and folded the tissue she'd been using. "I thought you wanted to land in jail."

Kate spun out the moment, the delicious tension, before telling her best friend her best secret. She waited for Julie to catch the anticipation. "If I'd been taken to jail then I wouldn't have been able to spend the afternoon with Mitch."

Sensing an even better story under that statement, Julie went fishing. "You spent the afternoon with Mitch?"

"Uh—huh." Kate nodded. Then she smiled. "Naked."

Julie's eyes widened and for a moment she looked destitute for words. Then she rubbed her palms together. "This is better than *The Young and the Restless!* Tell me everything!"

"Not everything," Kate demurred.

Julie cocked an eyebrow. "Everything. You know I've heard several rumors about Mitch McKee and I want to know the truth."

"You're a married woman," Kate countered, like it was an accusation.

"Married and pregnant. Doesn't mean I'm dead. How do you think I got in this condition, anyway? Now, tell me, you promised."

"What do you want to know?"

Julie pinkened slightly. "Well, does he have, you know..."

Kate was glad Julie's courage seemed to be sputtering. Her own ability to tell her friend *everything* was in serious jeopardy. "Does he have what?"

"Is he...well-endowed?"

"Julie Blake! I can't believe you are asking about the endowments of your husband's friend. What would Cal say?"

"Cal's not here right now and I'm asking you. I've heard all sorts of things about Mitch and this is the first opportunity to find out the truth."

"Well, as your on-the-scene reporter, who has only a modest amount of experience with such things, I'd say he's well-endowed."

Julie went silent then, maybe rethinking her insistence on a report. "Are you happy? About the afternoon, I mean?" she asked finally.

Kate relaxed and met her friend's gaze. "It was the most incredible afternoon of my life."

MITCH KNEW when to throw in the towel. Kate had practically taken over his life since she'd cruised into town in her gold Mercedes. No matter how hard he'd tried to avoid it, she'd gotten to him...again. Then, when she'd announced that he should show up at her room later after the cocktail party—for reunion graduates only—he hadn't even put up a fight.

He was already a lost cause and his only hope was that Kate didn't recognize it yet. Without any obvious effort on her part, she'd slipped under his skin, into his blood, into his heart. He was a goner as far as Katie Sutherland was concerned. For all the good it would do him.

He'd go to her room—hell, he'd wait in her car—if that meant he could have time with her. Especially if they could be alone. His tough-guy reputation be damned. He'd never felt this way about anything or anyone before. He wanted to protect her, to shake some sense into her, to ease her on her back and keep her there for about a week. He'd take everything she had to give him as long as she was here to give it.

Because he knew she'd go. Back to her life in San Francisco, her job, her friends. And he'd have to deal with the empty place she'd ripped into his life.

She'd kissed him in front of her father. That told him she was still up to her plans to make daddy notice. Well, the old man had noticed all right, but Mitch didn't care what he thought. He just wished Kate had kissed him because she wanted to, because she had some feeling for him. Not because she wanted to shock her father.

But, hey, he'd known what she was about from the first night in town. Trouble. Since he was already up to his neck in it, in her, he might as well enjoy what he could. And he did enjoy her, every small twitch of her response, every sigh of release, every surprising turning of the tables. He'd go to her tonight, and love her until she couldn't forget him. No matter where she went or who she loved in the future.

He knew how to cause trouble, better than Kate Sutherland. They both might go up in flames, but it would be the most memorable fire in Chapel, Tennessee.

THE BANNER READ, Welcome Graduates Of Shelby High School, Chapel, Tennessee.

Kate put her arm around Julie's expanded waistline and hugged her. "Well, here goes, into the abyss."

Julie laughed and returned her hug before pulling her toward the welcome table. "Surely it won't be that bad."

An hour later, Kate decided it wasn't *that* bad, as Julie had said. It wasn't that good either.

Over cocktails and benign music, the group seemed perfectly civilized, until you listened in on the conversations of a few small cliques which had formed. With no husbands, wives or dates present, the same friends who had stuck together years before gravitated back to each other. And, it seemed as though they reverted to their old high-school personas as well. Most of the people attending either seemed surprised by the accomplishments of the other graduates, or irritated by them. Some of the "least likely-to-succeeds" had done quite well, thank you.

Kate decided sticking with your friends wasn't a bad idea. And since her only friend in high school had been Julie, the two of them made the rounds together. She'd almost relaxed when they ran into four girls, now women, who between them had been dishing out enough disparaging remarks to script a few episodes of *The Jerry Springer Show*.

"Why Julie, my lord, is that baby overdue? You

look like you could go into labor any moment," one of them said as they approached.

Kate stared at the woman's name tag trying to remember her. Karen Whitlow. No luck. She did remember one of the women with Karen, however, and knew this close encounter could likely get worse.

"How many will this be?" Lindsey Dickerson asked sweetly. Lindsey had always been something at Shelby High: a cheerleader or president of the student council or some other high-profile position achieved by popularity rather than skill. Kate had kept to herself, gone to class and studied, but the few unavoidable dealings she'd had with Lindsey Dickerson were forced and cold. Not the kind of person you'd want to sign your yearbook.

"This is my first," Julie answered with an angelic smile on her face. Kate had to hand it to her, she looked unshakeable. Maybe pregnancy helped center her, or maybe it gave her a better perspective on the important things in life. Just the same, Kate wished Cal was here to scare off these harpies, like he'd taken care of her at The Raven.

Not to mention Mitch.

Lindsey turned her attention to Kate then, as if Julie's life wasn't important enough to sustain a conversation. "And look at you, Katherine. My, you've changed since you moved to California. I hear they have a lot of good doctors out there. Maybe you could recommend one?"

Kate had purposely worn a demure, downright boring cocktail dress for the evening. She hadn't wanted to draw attention, not after the week she'd recently lived through. She'd have all the attention she could handle later when Mitch discovered what she'd worn, or failed to wear, under this dress.

"I'm sure there are good doctors everywhere, Lindsey." Kate looked at Julie and arched an eyebrow before adding, "Julie's doctor is excellent."

A slight twitter went through the group, but Lindsey wasn't dissuaded. "I've heard that you're unhampered by children or a husband. That job of yours must be a doozie." She leaned closer as if they were about to share a secret. "You know, my husband asked me to ask you—" she gave a slight don't-blame-me shrug "—just how much does that job of yours pay anyhow?"

Kate's grip on her glass of wine nearly made her hand shake. The wild girl had the overpowering urge to toss the drink in Lindsey's face. She felt Julie's worried gaze on her, thought of her friend's pregnant poise and managed to rustle up a smile. She leaned close to Lindsey, but as the other woman had done, she spoke loud enough for everyone in the group to hear. "Well, you just tell your husband that I'd be happy to discuss salaries with him. His and mine. Have him leave a message on my voice mail."

A moment of shocked silence followed.

"Oh look, there's Ronnie Williams, I haven't seen him since we put the yearbook together," Julie said and grabbed Kate's arm, pulling her across the room. "Bye," she said as an afterthought to Lindsey and the others.

Kate tried not to laugh—she really did. But when she looked back at Lindsey's angry face she felt one great, unladylike guffaw rising inside her. She couldn't wait to tell Mitch.

With one arm locked in Kate's and the other clamped onto the unsuspecting Ronnie Williams, Julie didn't stop until the three of them were near the opposite wall of the room from Lindsey and certain disaster.

Kate was still laughing when she glanced over Julie's head and spotted Mitch.

He was standing in the foyer of the large room, obviously having talked his way past the local librarian who was running the welcome table. He hadn't even been forced to wear a name tag as all the rest of them had.

He made no move to enter the room, even though he'd obviously been watching her. Kate's heartbeat picked up pace as it always had when Mitch was around. Feeling buoyed by her recent coup with Lindsey, Kate gave him a slow, seductive once-over. He wasn't wearing his trademark jeans tonight. In deference to the resort, he'd dressed in dark blue Dockers and a long-sleeved shirt open at the collar. No jacket, but he still looked every bit the casual country gentleman.

The thought that Mitch McKee, who didn't even wear a uniform for the city council, would go out of his way to dress for her reunion made Kate's heart beat even faster than before. That, and imagining what was going to happen in her room later. All she could think of was getting inside those clothes.

"I see you're easily distracted," Julie said.

"Huh?" Kate replied, bringing her attention back to the conversation.

Julie looked past her. "Don't worry, he's on his way over here."

Mitch crossed the room with one goal in mind. He wouldn't rush her, but he wanted Kate to himself in a room with a huge bed, on the double. It had nearly driven him crazy to stay away from her this long.

Nodding to some of the people he knew as he passed, he didn't try to make conversation. He reached Kate, and instead of pulling her into his arms as his body wanted, he touched the small of her back briefly with his hand as he said hello.

"Mitch, you know Ronnie, don't you?" Julie said.

"Sure," he replied and offered his hand.

"Chief," Ronnie acknowledged.

"How are things going over at the newspaper?" Mitch asked, making the small talk he'd sworn he'd avoid.

"Good," Ronnie said. "You know we're getting ready to build that new annex on the west side. I don't suppose you could put in a good word to the council about our building permits?"

Mitch smiled. He knew Ronnie wouldn't have any problems with the council. He raised one hand. "Don't look at me. I'm law enforcement, not zoning."

Just then, Kate entwined her fingers with his other hand. He squeezed her hand briefly and realized her fingers were trembling. Amid the noise and the conversations in the room, Mitch could feel his heart beat slow and hard.

Julie seemed to read his mind. "Well, I guess you guys have to go."

Bless you, Julie Blake. Mitch looked at Kate in question. She seemed reluctant.

"I can't leave you here all alone," she said to Julie.

With a smile, Julie gave Ronnie's arm a playful punch. "Ronnie will look after me, won't you?"

"You know I will," he answered. Then seeing his advantage, he asked, "Hey, does Cal still have that old boat trailer? I told him I'd buy it from him if he decided to let it go."

Kate cut into Ronnie's pitch, poking him in the chest to get his complete attention. "Don't you let those...those *witches* pick on her." Then she spoke to Julie. "Cal's coming to pick you up, right?"

Julie laughed again at Ronnie's confused expression, then patted Kate's arm. "Thanks, Mom," she joked. "You two have fun. I'll be fine."

As Mitch steered Kate from the room, he was almost afraid to ask. "What was that all about?"

Kate chuckled and said, "I'll tell you later. It was one of my finer bitchy moments. Maybe my only bitchy moment," she confessed.

They were nearly to do the door and freedom when Mitch heard a woman call his name.

"Is that Mitch McKee?"

He wouldn't have stopped but he'd already hesitated long enough for it to be obvious he'd heard.

When he turned, he felt Kate's hand squeeze his in a death grip before letting go.

The woman marched right up to them. "You must remember me, Lindsey Dickerson?"

"Uh..." The name sounded vaguely familiar. He turned to see if Kate might know her and decided from the look on her face, he needed to get her out of there. "Hi, nice to see you. We were just on our way out." He turned but the woman persisted.

"Surely you're not leaving so soon?"

Mitch searched for something polite to say since he didn't know if this was one of Kate's friends. Kate opened her purse and seemed to be ignoring the woman.

"We really—" he began.

"—have to go," Kate finished. She wagged her room key in the woman's face. "We're going to my room to have wild sex and room service. Beats the hell out of Muzak and Swedish meatballs."

Mitch watched the woman's mouth open and close twice before following Kate, who had set out for the door once again, this time with a decided sway in her backside.

"You're not drunk, are you?" Mitch asked, knowing the answer.

"No, I'm not," Kate answered sounding offended. "The wild girl in me has just had enough of some things."

In the hallway leading to the lobby, Mitch stopped, forcing Kate to turn and face him. He ran his hands up her bare arms. "She hasn't had enough of me, has she?" he asked, keeping his mouth within kissing distance of hers.

Her face tilted upward and all signs of anger disappeared. Her eyes trapped him with a gaze so sultry he felt the heat from his collar to his shoes. "Uh-uh," she murmured, shaking her head. Her hands slid up the front of his shirt as she licked her lips. "I've barely gotten a taste of you. I intend to have all eight courses."

"Eight?" he asked as her mouth touched his.

"We can make up a few, can't we?" she answered against his lips.

12

THEY MADE IT to the room in record time. Mitch decided it was a miracle they still had their clothes on when they got there. But as soon as they were both safely inside, alone, with the door locked, time seemed to slow and stretch. They had all night, Mitch reminded himself as he watched his natural-born hellion turn shy on him.

She fidgeted with the light switches, told him to have a seat, then tried to decide where. It was almost as though they were new to each other. Like the hot afternoon they'd spent together a few hours before had been a dream.

He finally caught her in his arms and just held her. "Is this the same woman who almost made love to me in the hallway a few minutes ago?"

Kate sighed and slumped against him. "This trip home has been such a crazy time. I can't believe I announced that you and I were going to have wild sex and room service."

Mitch chuckled and pushed his fingers into her hair. "Now that's the one part of the evening, so far, that I enjoyed the hell out of. Although after the shenanigans of this week, I shouldn't encourage you."

Kate raised her chin to tuck her face against his

neck. "I know. It's like I've discovered a whole new side of me that's been hiding in the background. Being wild sounds like so much fun, but it's actually a little scary."

Mitch thought back to the night at The Raven and felt like telling her she should never be wild again, purely for his own peace of mind. But up on that stage, facing down a roomful of people with next to nothing on, she'd been so beautiful, so damn full of fire. He had already admitted to himself that the wild part of her had nearly made him crazy, but he couldn't tell her. Not if he expected to have any stabilizing effect on the situation. He went for the logical approach.

"I think finding the wildness inside yourself is important—it enables you to take chances, test your own limits. But, like anything else, you have to know how to slow the velocity, how to enjoy the rush without getting completely out of control." He tilted his head at her. "Maybe you should enlist in the marines—that's what tempered my wild streak."

Kate pulled back to look in his eyes. "Ha, ha, ha," she said, making it clear she wasn't impressed with his sense of humor. Then she shrugged. "I wasn't out of control. The only reason I said the sex thing to Lindsey was because she'd been catty to Julie earlier in the evening. I wanted to say something to shock her and all her friends. Let them talk about me, not about Julie."

"Does that mean we aren't going to have wild sex and room service?" Mitch asked, doing his best to keep a straight face and pretend deep disappointment.

A swift open-handed shove in the solar plexus was his answer. Instead of fighting, he surrendered and fell backward onto the bed. Kate leaned over him with a sexy smile.

"You want wild?"

When he nodded, she said, "You got it."

She offered her hand to pull him to a sitting position, then repositioned him with his back against the pillows. She removed his shoes and socks then contemplated his clothes for one long lingering moment before dropping that line of thought. She turned down the lights in the room, then fiddled with the music system until she found the right, bluesy jazz music.

Before Mitch could catch his runaway anticipation, Kate began to dance.

For Kate, the feeling of impending nakedness had an entirely different effect this time. The wild girl wanted to dance, to strip for Mitch. And Kate wanted to experience the rush of looking into his eyes and seeing the heat caused by her—by Kate Sutherland. She wanted to finish what she'd begun at The Raven, only this time the show would be for one person— one man.

She closed her eyes for a moment to find the "groove" of the music as the deejay had instructed. She moved with the rhythm easier this time, her body already primed for what she was about to do. She ran her hands over the simple black dress she'd worn for an evening of conversation and felt bare skin beneath. Skin that would soon be touched by Mitch's warm hands. A sizzle of excitement raised the stakes.

She opened her eyes as her palms skimmed over her breasts and met Mitch's gaze. He seemed perfectly at ease, except for the deep rise and fall of his chest and the challenging expression on his face. She could almost hear his thoughts like she'd heard the men's catcalls in The Raven.

"Come on, baby."

"Do it."

"Take it off."

Kate would do it for Mitch, and everything about his posture said he wanted all she had to offer. The rush of sexual power almost made her dizzy. She arched her back and unzipped the dress.

In a stalling movement, Kate turned her bare back to him and allowed the dress to fall off her shoulders. There was total silence from behind her, but Kate knew he was watching; she could almost feel his gaze like a warm hand. With a playful smile, she turned toward him and allowed the dress to slither down to her hips.

Perhaps unable to stay still much longer or, more likely, wanting to participate, Mitch unbuttoned his shirt with unhurried movements. Kate watched as he dragged it upward, then off. He tossed it over a chair near the bed.

Kate decided there was something different about stripping for a half-naked man. Definitely more exciting when the man was Mitch McKee. She danced closer to give him a good look at her black lace demi-bra before she got down to serious business. She pushed the dress over her hips and let it slide to the floor at her feet.

Mitch seemed to freeze in place. Kate smiled as she ran her hands over her bare hips then crossed them to demurely cover what she'd wanted him to discover. She'd dredged up the garter belt and stockings but had left off the panties.

One of Mitch's hands reached out to touch her hip and Kate danced out of reach. If anticipation was everything, then she intended for Mitch to get the full treatment tonight. After all, he'd tortured her at his leisure when they'd been at the lake.

Sinking back into the mesmerizing music, Kate levered off her shoes and would have begun removing her stockings if Mitch hadn't stood up. He withdrew a flat package from his pocket and tossed it onto the night table. Condoms. The reality of what they were about to do shivered through Kate. If they'd pretended to be seventeen-year-olds that afternoon, they were unquestionably adults tonight. Surprised into waiting to see what else he intended to do, she watched as he, without taking his gaze from hers, unzipped his slacks and pushed them off along with his briefs.

Suddenly the would-be stripper had to face the disconcerting fact that her audience was more naked than she was. Before she could react to anything except the obvious arousal her dance had solicited, Mitch caught her in a bear hug and picked her up.

He tossed her on the bed then followed her down.

"Hey," she complained halfheartedly, "I wasn't done yet."

"How 'bout—" Mitch kissed her on the mouth, then on the center of her chest "—we do the rest together?"

An old niggling of self-doubt darkened the moment. "Didn't you like my strip?" Kate asked, beginning to feel like a total fool for thinking she could be wild and carry it off.

Mitch leaned back and held her gaze for several beats of her heart. "Honey, you were killin' me. That's why I had to touch you." He waited a full thirty seconds to see if she intended to argue.

Kate decided against arguing. Why argue when she'd gotten what she wanted, in spades? She raised her arms and looped them around his neck. "You look very alive to me, head to toe," she teased.

Proving her point, he took no interval for torture this time. With efficient fingers, he set to work on removing the rest of her sexy wardrobe, and in less than three minutes she was as naked as he was— skin-to-skin, mouth-to-mouth. Then he kissed her like a man who wanted to own the memory of every kiss she'd ever shared, staking his claim so that no one else had a chance to outdo him.

And Kate kissed him back, alternately offering her lips, her tongue. But then he moved lower, licking down the length of her neck, before kissing the wetness left behind. Her breasts became his goal and, within a few moments, the heat of his tongue and the sweet suction of his lips had her squirming.

Mitch used his teeth to titillate Kate's nipple and she gasped in a breath of surprise. Her nails dug into his back, however, exposing the level of arousal she'd reached. He couldn't wait much longer himself.

He hadn't been kidding when he'd said she was killing him. At the moment, he found himself balanced on a pinnacle he'd never reached before. He'd let down all his defenses and allowed Kate to get to him. Physically, watching her strip in a show for one, had set him on fire, but her willingness and trust had also made something inside of him weak with another kind of wanting. The physical part he could satisfy, for both of them. The other part would have to take care of itself.

Mitch slowly left her breasts and moved up to look into Kate's eyes. The sultry expression on her face made the wanting stronger. He lightly kissed her lips as he ran one hand down over her belly and slid his palm over her sex. Then he waited.

"Are you ready?" he whispered.

Instead of answering with words, Kate arched her hips and opened her thighs for his fingers. The whimper she made when he pushed a finger inside her made his erection pulse. Withdrawing his finger, he reached for the package of condoms. *Protection.* He would protect Kate from anything, even himself.

The wayward thought of Kate big, like Julie, with his baby nearly made him drop the package. *Get a hold of yourself, McKee. You're having sex, not making ba-*

bies. Funny, he'd never put those thoughts together before Kate.

Kate made a sound of impatience and Mitch shrugged away any thought except the urgency of what was happening between them. He put on the condom and nudged her knees apart.

As Mitch pushed inside her, Kate cried out—not from pain but from pure need. Between thinking about this night for hours, and hatching her own plan to seduce Mitch, her mind and body were at such a fever pitch the waiting had become unbearable.

Now Mitch had filled that need and she didn't care what he did to her as long as he didn't leave her.

Mitch's hands moved up to trap her own near her head and he held her steady as he set a slow, pulsing rhythm. Kate wanted more. She tried to drag her hands free, to urge him to go faster. But he held her immobile.

"Mitch..." she pleaded. But again he denied her.

Then, nearing a mindless state, Kate did the only other thing she could do. She raised her legs and clamped them around his hips.

With a groan of defeat, Mitch plunged into her, harder and faster, and as Kate left the ground for that rarer air of climax, she smiled.

"Yessss."

After several taught moments, the coiled wire of sexual hunger relaxed, leaving Kate to free float in her now satiated body. Held down by Mitch's welcome weight, she nevertheless felt lighter, unfettered and infinitely better than she had moments before, than she had since she'd last been with Mitch, in fact.

When he braced his arms to relieve her of his full weight and looked into her eyes, she blurted out, "That was incredible."

Still slightly out of breath, the serious set of his mouth twisted with a smile. "Hey, that's supposed to be my line." He kissed her nose before untangling his hips from her legs and rolling to one side. "How about...that was better than catching Grandaddy Bass twice in one day?" He snuggled her close to him and yanked the sheet over them both.

"Great," Kate replied, knowing he was teasing her, but playing indignant anyway. "Now I'm being compared to a fish!"

"Not just any fish," Mitch drawled. His arms tightened around her to keep her from getting away. "Nothing less than the biggest, wiliest, oldest fish in the lake."

Kate gave him a quelling look. "I think you'd better stop while you're *not* ahead."

"You're right," Mitch agreed, then he watched her for a moment before going on. "Truthfully? Tonight may have been one of the best in my memory. How's that?"

Kate's feigned indignance disappeared. She concentrated on the sound of his voice and the exact words—she wanted to remember everything about this night for the rest of her days. She'd never dreamed Mitch McKee would think of her as anything but little Katie Sutherland.

"Really?" Hungry for details, she asked, "What part did you like the best?" For a moment, she regretted the question because it sounded so sophomoric. If he laughed at her, she'd be forever sorry she'd opened her mouth.

Mitch must have seen the anxiety in her eyes because he didn't laugh. He scooted her up further on the bed, so her head rested on his shoulder before answering.

"I think the part I liked the best was watching you strip," he began.

Kate felt a thrill of elation that she'd finally gotten the whole stripping thing together. She'd managed to be brave enough and sexy enough to seduce a hard case like Mitch McKee. Maybe going to The Raven hadn't been a totally stupid idea. If she'd only known that in high school...

"Not for the reason you think," he continued.

Kate's back-patting session screeched to a halt. "What do you mean?"

"I mean—" he kissed her nose again "—it wasn't the strip so much as the fact that you were doing it. Not that you aren't a beautiful and sexy woman," he quickly added. Then he frowned, as if searching for the right words.

"The strip was exciting because you wanted to please me." He raised a hand to the empty room. "Just me. And, the most important part, you trusted me. Nobody takes their clothes off in front of another human being unless there's a level of trust." He used one hand to turn her face to his for a lingering kiss.

"Of course, being inside you is as close to heaven as I'll ever get," he said, against her lips.

Kate's sentiments were much the same about having Mitch inside her. For the first time, the logical part of her brain skipped ahead from the moment. Skipped ahead to the day after tomorrow when she would be leaving Chapel, Tennessee, and Mitch behind. A sharp, crushing dose of reality made her throat tight. She couldn't have spoken if her life depended on it.

"I used to watch you, you know, in high school," Mitch went on. A slight smile softened his mouth as he seemed to be looking back into the past. "Whenever I went into the library, or the cafeteria, I could almost feel your hungry eyes on me. I'd look around until I found you." He smiled outright and gazed at Kate. "You'd always look away like a scared rabbit. Then I could watch you all I wanted because you'd have your nose stuck in a book." He sighed and chuckled. "Hell, you were the object of more than a few of my masturbation fantasies."

Kate found her voice then. She couldn't believe he'd wanted her all those years ago when she would have given anything to be his. "Why didn't you ever talk to me?"

His smile disappeared and he sighed. "Because of your daddy and who I was. Because of your mother dying and my mother trying to keep me out of jail. All of that. I might have been a little scared of you too, but don't tell anybody."

Without warning, Kate rolled until she was lying

on top of him, head to foot, with her arms braced on his chest. "Afraid of me? Why in heaven's name were you afraid of me?"

Mitch smiled up into her challenging eyes. "Well now, if you'd come at me like this—" he ran his hands over her bare back and butt "—I wouldn't have had time to think about it."

Kate framed his face with her hands. "I'm serious. Why did you say you were afraid?"

Looking like he regretted the words already, he reluctantly answered, "You were always smart, Kate. And you had the opportunities. It wouldn't have taken you long to outdistance someone like me. I didn't want to have you, then watch you walk out of my life."

Not unlike what she intended to do now, Kate realized. Before she could wrap her mind around that concept and what Mitch was trying to tell her, the phone rang. Without changing her position, Kate reached for the receiver.

"Hello?"

"Is this Kate?" a male voice asked.

"Yes, who is this?"

"This is John Dealey, Mayor Dealey."

Kate frowned at Mitch before sliding off him and sitting up. "I'm glad you called. I wanted to say how sorry I am—" Then it occurred to her how odd it was for him to be phoning so late. "Mayor? What's wrong? Why are you calling? Has something happened to my father?"

"No, no. Calm down. Nothing has happened to your father, yet."

"What do you mean yet?"

Mitch moved to sit up next to her. He rested a warm hand on her thigh.

"You know I mentioned that you and I should get together. But then there was that unfortunate accident at the golf course. I think now you owe me some kind of recompense."

Kate drew in a deep breath. She couldn't believe the man's gall. "Mayor, have you been drinking? It's eleven o'clock at night, a little late for some kind of joke."

"I'm not joking. Either you make some time to spend with me privately or I'll tell your father all about your grand evening as a stripper. If I were your father, I would be deeply wounded that my flesh and blood had sunk so low."

Kate lost her temper then. "You are not my father, Mayor, although I'm sure you're my father's age. Tell him whatever you like and leave me alone." She hung up the receiver. Then, as an afterthought, she called the front desk and asked them to hold all calls until morning.

SOMETIME AFTER MIDNIGHT, Mitch and Kate were awakened by an insistent knock on Kate's hotel room door. Motioning for Kate to stay put, Mitch found his slacks and pulled them on before looking through the peephole into the hallway. To his amazement, Mayor

Dealey, sporting two black eyes, waited impatiently on the other side.

Kate had explained the phone call and that had seemed weird enough, but who would have thought the somewhat injured and very married Mayor would try to bully his way into Kate's room? Well, Mitch thought, he was in for a big surprise. He unhooked the door chain, turned the handle and swung the door wide.

"Evening, Mayor," Mitch said. Then he watched as the man looked him over from his bare feet, to bare chest, to tousled hair. "What can I do for you?"

"Kate?" the Mayor managed to squeak out.

"She's asleep right now. Want to leave a message?"

The mayor nodded.

"Fine," Mitch said. "You can leave it at the front desk." As Mitch turned to close the door, he couldn't resist one parting shot. "Does your wife know where you are?" Not waiting for an answer, he slammed the door.

13

THEY HAD BREAKFAST at the Blakes' house. Both Julie and Cal seemed pleased by the fact that Kate and Mitch had spent the night together. They didn't come right out and say it, however.

"You look happier than you oughta be," Cal said to Mitch as he and Kate sat down at the dining room table.

Happier... Mitch's mind produced a full color replay of slipping inside Kate the night before and pronouncing, *We fit together, tight and hot.* Yeah, you might say he was happy. He could feel his blood pressure rise at the memory. Without acknowledging what Cal had really meant, Mitch replied, "You look better than the mayor," and tapped a finger under his own unmarred eye.

"Yeah, well—" Cal gingerly patted the now greenish-blue bruise under his left eye "—mine was for a good cause."

"I don't think the phrase 'good cause' can be associated with our illustrious city leader," Mitch said. He sat back so that Julie could pour him a cup of coffee. "Mayor Dealey showed up at Kate's room last night, being a little more pushy than I can ignore."

"What?" Julie said, and quickly pulled up a chair

to hear the rest. She set the coffeepot on the place mat.

Mitch glanced at Kate, then said, "Seems he thinks he can scare her into going a few rounds with him."

"She already hit him in the nose with a golf ball," Julie observed. "He ought to quit while he's ahead."

Cal's big hand covered Julie's smaller one. "He's talking about sex, hon."

Julie's face scrunched up like she'd smelled something rotten. "Euuuuwwwww."

"Scare her...how?" Cal wanted to know. "Did he try to hurt her?"

"No," Mitch answered. He wouldn't want Kate to hear what he would do to anyone who tried to hurt her—not at the breakfast table anyhow. He'd learned some things in the marines that were better kept secret. "If he had, you'd be bailing me out of jail. Let's say when he came to her room, he was real surprised that I answered his knock on the door."

"He threatened to tell my father about my stiptease at The Raven," Kate supplied.

"But I thought you wanted your father to know," Julie said, confused.

Kate sighed. "I did, I guess. I don't know." Her gaze shifted to Mitch for a second, then back to Julie. "At this point, I don't really care one way or the other."

Julie seemed to think about that information for a moment. Then she picked up the coffeepot and signaled to Kate. "Come help me get breakfast together," she said.

Mitch knew a feminine conspiracy when he saw one brewing but he decided to stay out of it—although he did consider mentioning that the current trouble with the mayor had begun with just such a "plan." He watched as Kate and Julie disappeared into the kitchen, then shrugged his shoulders at Cal.

"You want to ride up to the lake and help me hook up that old boat trailer?" Cal asked.

KATE WAS CORNERED by Julie as soon as the swinging door closed behind them.

"This is sooo exciting," Julie said as she hugged Kate. "I just knew you and Mitch would hit it off if you just stopped—well, you know—if you just took a good look at each other."

Kate, conscious of Julie's oversize belly, gave her the best hug she could manage. "I'm not sure what to say," she smiled. "But as for Mitch and I hitting it off—" Her memory produced the image of her and Mitch, not five minutes after the mayor had left her room, making slow and heart-pounding love. "You could say that, I guess."

"He's got that look on his face," Julie pronounced as she opened the refrigerator.

"What look?"

Julie put a dozen eggs and a gallon of milk on the counter. "Get the bacon out of there, will you? You know, the *look*. A man gets the look when he's, oh, won the bass tournament, or when he's made a hole in one, or—" she shrugged "—when he's fallen in love."

Kate, who after retrieving the bacon had been in the process of getting herself a cup of coffee, stopped in the middle of pouring. "Love?"

"That's what I said," Julie informed her. "And before you tell me it's not true, let me ask you three questions. One, is he taking you to the reunion dance tonight?"

Kate finished pouring and nodded. "He said it was in case the mayor showed up."

Julie nodded sagely, before dropping an entire pound of bacon into a frying pan. "Men hate those things unless they themselves have a reason to be there." She made a face. "That reason usually has to do with picking up women, or causing trouble."

"Maybe he's just being polite," Kate said, but knew it sounded weak. Mitch was not the polite type unless he chose to be.

"Number two," Julie continued, "Has he mentioned five things he had to do today other than be with you?"

Kate was beginning to get nervous and she wasn't sure why, except that loving Mitch seemed like a much larger step than making love with him. "Well, no. He knew we were coming here for breakfast—after you called and woke us up, that is..."

"Okay. Here's the last one and the most important." Julie stopped and stared at her friend. "Has he asked you what time your flight is tomorrow?"

Unreasonably relieved, Kate rushed to answer. "No, he hasn't. See, if he was falling in love, he'd want to take me to the airport."

Julie shook her head sadly. "No, Kate. He hasn't asked about your flight because he doesn't want to think of you leaving." She waited a moment for the truth of her reasoning to sink in, then she went on. "Have you asked yourself those kinds of questions?"

Kate knew she was in deep trouble. Not that loving Mitch was a bad thing; it was just a surprise. She'd been so busy unwrapping the present of his undivided attention, she hadn't analyzed why everything they did together felt...right. She'd thought it had to do with being old acquaintances. But now, the magnitude of the gift he had offered far outshone anything from the past.

They weren't seventeen anymore. They had a lot more at stake by offering their hearts in the present than any two high-school kids. What had Mitch said? He didn't want to love her then have to let her go? Well, she didn't want to love him, then leave him, either.

"Don't panic," Julie interrupted her. "You'll know what to do when the time comes."

Shocked that Julie could read her thoughts so well, Kate said, "How did you—"

"Put some toast in, will you?" Julie asked, then she squeezed Kate's hand. "It's a pregnancy thing. I have my antennae out. Who knows? Soon I might be picking up radio signals from Antarctica."

IT FELT LIKE the longest day of her life, Kate decided. She and Julie had done all they could to make it interesting, but, for Kate, being away from Mitch was a hardship. After breakfast, he'd reluctantly allowed Cal to enlist his help to move an old boat trailer he'd been storing at the lake. When they'd pulled out, even Kate, who wasn't in Julie's condition, knew Mitch didn't really want to leave. But she hadn't known how to ask him to stay.

Instead of going back to the resort and participating in the organized reunion golf tournament—Kate had had enough golf—or the trout fishing tournament at the local stocked trout pond—what do you do with a trout in a hotel room?—Kate and Julie had gone shopping. Kate oohed and ahhed over every tiny pair of baby shoes Julie fell in love with, making a mental note to send her some for a shower gift. Every well-dressed baby should have at least five pairs, she figured.

But all the while, her mind was on Mitch.

They'd had lunch and stopped for ice cream before Julie dropped her off at the hotel with the final advice to give her brain a rest and follow her heart.

An hour later, Kate glanced at the clock again and sighed. It didn't seem to have moved. She'd already touched up her dress with the iron, showered and styled her hair. All she had left to do was put on her makeup and get dressed.

She dreaded the dance; after her less than dignified exit the night before, she didn't want to set eyes on Lindsey Dickerson again. But she couldn't wait to see Mitch. They had agreed to have dinner at the resort before doing their duty and attending the dance. She decided she'd had enough time away from him to calm down the sexual tension. Now she could pay attention to the emotion. She wanted to look into his eyes and see the truth, then she would decide what to do.

At precisely seven o'clock, the phone rang in her room. She checked out her reflection in the mirror as she reached for the receiver.

"Hey."

At the mere sound of his voice, a fiery thrill ran under her skin leaving a smoking trail. So much for calming down.

"Hey, yourself," she answered. She could hear the sounds of people in the lobby around him.

"You ready to eat?"

Food was very close to the last thing on her mind at that moment. "I'm hungry," she said, then felt heat rising up her neck. Playing the sexual game was new to her, but the outcome was as old as time.

"Would you rather have room service?" he asked and she could hear the smile in his words. She should have known she couldn't win the innuendo wars; he'd obviously had more practice.

Besides, they hadn't gotten around to ordering room service the night before. They'd been too busy with each other to be concerned with food. "I think we better eat in the dining room, otherwise I'll starve."

She heard a huff of laughter before he said, "Come on down here, then. I promise to wait for you."

On wobbly knees, Kate closed the door to her room and made her way to the lobby, all the way telling herself that her reaction to Mitch was a combination of an old crush and this crazy trip back home. She'd almost convinced herself when the elevator opened and she saw him directly across the hallway, dressed for the evening and holding a single red rose. It was the first time she'd ever seen him in a suit.

Kate's heart took several hard, hammering beats as she looked in his face. She felt like the sight of him had lifted her from the ground, and her heart had jumped to accommodate the change in altitude. Drop-dead gorgeous. The elevator doors started to close, requiring her to put out a hand to stop them. Still staring into his eyes, she took a deep breath and walked forward to meet her fate.

Mitch felt like swearing. He'd spent all day cussin' and sweatin' and working with Cal on that damned boat trailer when the only thing he'd wanted to do was be with Kate.

Hell.

Watching her walk toward him, dressed in a subtle but sexy, fire-engine red dress that probably cost more than he made in a month, he felt...unworthy. Damn, it had been years since he'd suffered that feeling. This time it was different though. It wasn't that he felt less than everyone else because of his father, or because of the low expectations for his future. It was because Kate loomed above them all and he'd had the nerve to put his hands on her.

He should be shot.

He didn't care.

As she neared, he picked up her sweet feminine

scent and had to clear his throat to make sure his reactions hadn't frozen his tongue. To hide his weakness, he kissed her lightly on the cheek and handed her the rose.

"You look beautiful," he said, feeling less than eloquent. Indicating the single flower, he added, "I thought we were a little past the corsage stage."

"Thank you, for the rose, and the compliment," she replied. Bringing the rose up to smell its perfume, she gave him a brazen head-to-toe appraisal. "You look pretty beautiful, yourself."

He took her arm, just so he could touch her, and headed them both toward the resort restaurant. "I'm not sure I've ever heard anyone describe me as either pretty or beautiful and you managed to get them both in one sentence. Are you sure you're with the right guy?"

She stopped, forcing him to look at her. Staring into her serious blue eyes held his complete attention.

"Oh yeah, I'm sure," she said.

Mitch found he didn't have a reply for that one except a heartfelt, but silent, thank God!

Dinner was torture.

Mitch watched Kate's hands as she cut her steak, he watched her mouth as she chewed and couldn't remember more than half the words she'd said.

He was worse than a buck in rut. All he wanted to do was push back from the table, lead her back to her hotel room, and continue what they'd started the day before. He wanted her more than any woman he'd ever known—hell, even the ones he didn't know.

A lost cause.

No one would ever believe it, but if he wasn't careful, he'd end up on his knees begging her to stay.

Mitch put down his fork and reached for his water glass. The one subject concerning Kate he hadn't wanted to think about had just sprung up and bit him. Kate would leave tomorrow.

The thought of it made his throat tight, too tight for a steak dinner. If he was lucky, maybe he'd choke to death right here and not have to face losing her. Hell. He was a war veteran, a gung-ho marine who could survive on bugs and branch water if he had to. But he wasn't sure how long he could make it without Kate now that he knew her. Now that he knew he loved her.

The guys in his old unit would laugh their asses off if they heard. Or, maybe they'd wish that just once in their long and uneventful lives they'd met one woman who could make them sweat long-distance.

"Is there something wrong with your steak, sir?" the waiter asked.

Mitch brought his mind back to his meal. He waved the man off. "No, it's fine." His gaze met Kate's. "I'm just not very hungry." *Not.*

Kate smiled as though she understood and the waiter left, whether he understood or not.

"I never asked whether you dance," Kate said. "Can you?"

The long list of school-sponsored dances that neither of them had attended echoed through his memory. He'd never asked Kate to a dance because that would have been a connection, a starting point for the two of them. And also because he believed her to be a smart girl who would say no to a troublemaker like himself.

"My mom taught me how to dance when I was about nine. She said she'd rather I dance with girls than be running with a bunch of hellion boys."

"Your mother was a very smart lady," Kate acknowledged.

"For all the good it did her," he said and placed his napkin over his plate. "Are you ready to show me off?"

Kate laughed and Mitch thought it was the most beautiful sound he'd heard in a long, long time.

"Can I talk you into doing a strip for the class of 1989?" she asked.

"Not in this lifetime."

THE EVENING began with an embarrassing slide show of old high-school photos, with someone crooning into the microphone, "Guess who?"

They'd already been given name badges adorned with yearbook portraits—except Mitch. He'd been conveniently absent on picture day so someone had dug up a shot from one of the cross-country events to put on his badge. It seemed to be no secret that he would attend the reunion; the small-town gossip mill had been working overtime and at light speed.

Kate didn't care. She was with Mitch and they'd found a table to share with Julie and Cal. Lindsey Dickerson had kept her distance and in a couple of hours she'd be spending another hot night with the man she—

"We missed you at the dinner, Katherine," a voice behind her said.

Kate swiveled and looked up into a face she recognized. "Why hello, Mr. Gardener." She'd been in his World History class. She extended her hand. "We had other plans and couldn't make the group dinner. You look just the same as I remember."

"I won't say the same about you. Why, you've blossomed into a beautiful young woman. Your father must be proud."

Her father. Always Terry Sutherland's daughter.

Moving past his comment, Kate turned to the others at the table. "Did you guys have Mr. Gardener for history?" She'd much rather step out of the center of attention.

When she introduced Mitch, Mr. Gardener swept a hand between the two of them and said, "My, how things have changed. Right, McKee?"

Mitch nodded but didn't reply and the wild girl stirred in Kate. She wanted to stand up face-to-face with Jerry Gardener as an adult and ask him exactly what he'd meant by that? But, unfortunately, she already knew what he meant, as she was sure Mitch did. It meant that the two of them, the daughter of the richest man in town and the troublemaker who'd raised hell throughout the county, would never live down their respective beginnings. Or the fact that they'd arrived at the reunion together.

It was almost a relief when the music began to play and Mr. Gardener wandered off.

"Can you believe they dug up Milli Vanilli?" Julie laughed in disbelief. "Talk about fifteen minutes of fame. We should dance out of sympathy."

She grinned at Cal and he simply said, "No."

As the evening progressed, the lights got dimmer, the music louder and there always seemed to be a line at the bar. Kate was feeling anonymous after speaking with the few people she'd actually known in school. The rest would have to entertain themselves. She felt free to ignore the crowd and concentrate on Mitch, especially when he guided her to the dance floor for a slow dance.

"You dance very well," Kate teased, then slithered her arms upward to encircle his neck and pressed herself closer.

"Are you determined to give them something to talk about?" Mitch said, near her ear. "Or are you trying to torture me?"

Stung by his comment, she leaned back to look into his eyes. "I don't care what they think. I was doing what I wanted to do—getting closer to you."

The smile he gave her nearly melted her panty hose. "Well, you come on, then." He pulled her close once more. Then he spoke into her ear again. "You can rest your beautiful chest against mine...anytime."

They danced until it became apparent to both of them that a room and a bed would soon be required. On the way off the dance floor, they ran into Julie and

Cal who seemed to be of the same mind only for different reasons.

"I tell you, if Cal has to explain what happened to his face one more time, I think I'll scream. Can't people mind their own business?" Julie huffed.

"Maybe I should start offering to show 'em exactly how I got my shiner," Cal said with a wicked smile.

"Don't start any fights now. We're on our way out," Mitch said.

"Us, too," Julie grimaced. "You know that little dancing baby on the Internet? Well, he or she is doing an Irish jig in my belly. I've had enough of a good time for one night."

The squeal of the microphone punctuated Julie's words and the four of them turned to look at the stage. Suddenly the lights came up and the music stopped.

Lindsey Dickerson stepped up to the microphone, wearing the perfect little sky-blue dress and a Cheshire-cat smile. "Hi. My name is Lindsey, for those of you who don't know. I hope everyone's having loads of fun," she said.

"People who are that perky should be tranquilized," Julie said to Kate behind her hand.

"I see some of you are leaving, but I hope you'll stay a few more moments. We have several door prizes and awards to give out," Lindsey announced.

They sat through the door prizes without winning. But when the awards part of the ceremony began, Kate got nervous.

There was the usual "Person who changed the

most since high school," then, "Person who changed the least." Kate had just begun to relax when they got to "Person most likely to start a family," and Julie's name was called. Kate, Mitch and Cal cheered loudly as Julie, in her best pregnant waddle, went forward to collect her large stuffed teddy bear.

"Now," Lindsey said, "we have one final award."

Kate squeezed Mitch's hand in preparation to leave.

"It's a dual award, and quite an unusual combination as you'll see. It's for "The graduate most likely to succeed," in tandem with "The graduate most likely to be arrested."

A startled twitter went around the room as Lindsey stretched out the moment. "The award goes to...Kate Sutherland!"

The people at the tables around Kate weren't sure whether to clap or not.

"I'm not going up there," she said to Mitch.

Lindsey shaded her eyes as though she couldn't see beyond the spotlights. "Kaa-te? Are you out there?"

"Cal? Can you throw this bear hard enough to hit that bit—" Julie stopped and rubbed her belly as if she couldn't swear in front of their in utero child. "To hit that busybody in the head?" she finished.

"Kate, come on now, don't be shy." Lindsey was obviously not giving up until Kate acknowledged the award.

"Want me to go get it?" Mitch asked.

The wild girl stirred in Kate and she awarded

Mitch a sizzling look. "I'm saving you for later. I'll go." Gritting her teeth, she pushed back her chair.

"Uh-oh," Julie said.

Kate had had enough of this reunion, enough of the small minds and hearts of Chapel, Tennessee, and waaaay more than enough of Lindsey Dickerson. She did her best hip-swaying sashay across the dance floor and, within a few moments, she stood face-to-face with her nemesis on stage.

Lindsey welcomed her with a completely fake smile of congratulations. "The prize is a bottle of champagne for your success—" her smile melted into a smirk "—and a nice strong file to saw through the bars." Laughing as though she'd actually made a joke, Lindsey handed over the bottle, with the file dangling from it by a red ribbon, to Kate.

Kate held the bottle up, as though she appreciated being humiliated. Then she turned her attention to her tormentor.

"Why, Lindsey, that's a lovely dress you have on." Kate winced as her voice was picked up by the microphone but that couldn't be helped. "Is it silk?"

Lindsey's hand fluttered along the expensive material of her dress as if to say, "You mean, this old thing?" "Yes, actually, it is. It's a Donna Karan. I bought it on my last trip to New York."

"I see." Kate slipped the file out of its ribbon and went to work on the wire of the champagne cork. Out of the corner of her eye, she saw Mitch push to his feet as if he had read her mind.

Too late, she thought triumphantly as the wire fell

away. She smiled at Lindsey and tossed the file onto the podium, giving the bottle a good shake.

As Kate positioned her thumbs to pop the cork, she turned to face Lindsey and caught the look of horror twisting her features. Kate hesitated, relaxing her grip on the bottle. Perhaps she was taking this a bit far, she thought.

Then Lindsey narrowed her eyes, saying, "Don't even think about it, you spoiled brat." And Kate let the cork fly.

Mitch reached the podium just as the woman giving the award screamed. He tried to snatch the bottle out of Kate's hands, but laughing, she stepped out of his reach, raising the bottle and then taking a victory swig of champagne. It was all he could do not to laugh along with her, but since he was chief of police he felt he needed to act like it.

Some of the people in the room, like the three women who had clustered around the victim, didn't find Kate's antics funny. The rest were hooting their approval, much like the crowd at The Raven. Mitch finally managed to get the wild girl down and away from the podium but she seemed to be reveling in the moment, offering champagne to him and anyone else in the vicinity.

He turned his back on the award giver which might have been a mistake, because, a moment later, she was next to him, screaming at Kate.

"Look what you did to my dress! I should have you arrested right now. Or sue you!" she screeched.

Kate seemed beyond stopping. "Sue me if you

want," she said. "But it'll be quicker if you just send my daddy the bill for the dress." She glanced at the other woman's wet hair and fought back a grin. "I'm not paying for the hair, though. Whoever did it should be shot."

"That's it," Mitch said, taking Kate's arm. "We're out of here." He tugged the champagne bottle out of her hands and set it on the nearest table, then aimed her toward the exit.

"I'm sorry, Mitch, I just couldn't help it. She—"

Deputy Les had entered the room and stopped their forward progress halfway across the ballroom. Just what Mitch needed, another crisis to handle when all he wanted to do was get Kate out of this room and into hers.

"Are you here to arrest me?" Kate asked the deputy without surprise or concern.

Facing the wild girl again, Deputy Les looked wary and hesitant, so Mitch attempted to deflect Kate's antics.

"Kate. He can't be here for you, there wasn't time to call it in," Mitch said. Then he asked the deputy, "Why *are* you here?"

Deputy Les hemmed and hawed for a moment, not really paying attention to the uproar around him. "Actually, Chief, I *am* here for Miz Sutherland."

Mitch felt poleaxed. Had the deputy been in the parking lot?

"What's the charge?"

"Assault."

Both Kate and Mitch spoke at once. "Assault?"

Then Kate twisted in his grasp. "I never touched you, Lindsey! Since when is being doused with champagne called assault?"

Mitch tightened his grip on Kate's arm. He heard the other woman reply but his attention was on his deputy. He had a bad feeling about this.

"Who signed the complaint?" Mitch asked.

Deputy Les looked more miserable than a city official should. "The mayor did, Chief. He ordered me to come over and get her, and take her out in handcuffs."

"Let me get this straight," Mitch said through his clamped teeth. "The mayor, being of sound mind and not under the influence of drugs or alcohol, sent you over here to arrest my date?"

Deputy Les shifted on his feet, looking for all the world like he wanted to run. Finally, he gave a jerky nod and answered, "Yes, sir."

Even Kate had been surprised into silence. People were beginning to move closer to try to hear the conversation and Lindsey Dickerson, the offended MC, had noticed a uniform and set out across the room saying, "Officer? Officer!"

Whether to get away from Lindsey or to somehow escape the reunion from hell, Kate shrugged and held out her hands to be cuffed.

Deputy Les looked from her to Mitch. Mitch didn't leave any doubt.

"Don't even think about it." He took Kate's arm and moved forward, leaving Deputy Les to follow them out.

14

"WHERE ARE WE GOING?" Kate asked.

Mitch, who'd been driving in silence since they'd left the resort, rubbed a hand down his face to try to get his temper under control.

"To the courthouse," he said.

After a long stretch of silence, Kate said, "I'm sorry."

With a sigh, Mitch hit the brakes and pulled to the side of the road. He tried to ignore the fact that Deputy Les, who was following them in a patrol car, also pulled to the side. Mitch took the truck out of gear and set the brake. Then, he turned to face Kate.

"Honey, this isn't your fault."

She looked on the verge of tears and the thought of his wild girl crying made him want to kill the mayor, slowly and painfully.

"I'm the one who hit the mayor with the golf ball." She swiped away a trail of wetness on her cheek. "I'm the one who did the strip, and who doused Lindsey." She sniffed and gazed up at him with absolute trust. "Do you think I need counseling?"

Mitch searched for the right words. Hell, what did he know about the minds of women? He took a deep breath and went forward with the only thing that made sense to him. "I think you need an anchor," he said.

"You mean, tied around my neck before I'm thrown in the lake?" Kate replied, doing her best to show a sense of humor as a new rush of tears spilled down her cheeks.

Mitch frowned to reinforce the seriousness of the occasion. "No, an anchor like—" He desperately searched his mind for an example. "Like Cal."

"Cal?" Kate nearly smiled. "You mean I need a big ol' boy with a shiner to hold me down?"

Mitch ignored her attempts at humor; he knew it was a dodge. "I mean in your life. Cal is Julie's anchor. You don't have your family, not really. And your job, no matter how important and well-paid, must not be enough to make up for that. You need something or someone in your life that makes you feel satisfied. Something worth your complete attention and commitment." Not really sure where that speech had originated, Mitch had the sudden insight that the words he'd just spoken to Kate were relevant to his own life as well. He hated when that happened.

Behind them, Deputy Les flicked the lights on his cruiser on and off, signaling to get them moving along.

Mitch hit the steering wheel with enough force to make Kate jump. The mayor had better stay out of arm's reach or he just might experience how uncivilized the grown-up version of Chapel's bad boy could be. He put the truck in gear and squealed the tires as he hit the pavement again.

"Sorry, Kate. I didn't mean to scare you. I've had about enough of this. And it'll be settled tonight."

By the time they reached the courthouse, Kate felt as wilted as the rose Mitch had given her earlier. The evening had begun with such promise and, now, because of her juvenile plans to shock her father, everything she'd wanted had unraveled.

And here Mitch was, defending her again. She thought he must be beyond tired of having to deal with repercussions of her behavior. Beyond tired of her father, of the people around her like Lindsey Dickerson. Way beyond tired of everything about her...except the sex.

She knew he wasn't tired of the sex. Even in her sorry state of mind, the idea of Mitch wanting her inside and out made her belly feel warm and pliant. Like her skin could remember his touch, teasing her, soothing her, making her crazy. She studied his tight-jawed profile as he steered the car into the chief's parking place. If not for her genius for trouble making, they'd be in her room right now, naked, nasty and happy.

Happy...

Mitch killed the engine and looked at her. "Are you ready?" he asked.

"As I'll ever be," she answered, feeling that wave of loss again. This had been her last night to spend with Mitch and now it had been ruined.

The mayor was waiting at the dispatch desk when Mitch, Kate and Deputy Les entered the building. Dealey's appearance, with two clownlike black circles around his eyes, might have been funny if Mitch hadn't been so angry. He didn't bother with the usual booking procedure, he went straight for the mayor.

"What the hell are you trying to do, John?" Mitch asked, getting right in the man's face.

Smart enough to recognize real trouble when he saw it, the mayor edged back a step, then his gaze darted to Deputy Les, as if he might help in a pinch. In a plea for sympathy, he raised a hand to his nose.

"Now, don't do anything stupid, McKee. This doesn't involve you. This is between me and her."

"You mind telling me what exactly is between you and Kate?"

"Why—why—" He tried to move around Mitch but only got a half step. He pointed toward Kate. "She hit me in the face with a golf ball. She could have killed me."

"It was an accident," Mitch countered.

"No—" The mayor swallowed nervously. "She did it on purpose."

"When did you decide that?" Mitch demanded. "I was at the country club and spoke to the witnesses. Did you decide to change your tune before or after you came to her hotel room last night?"

"You're going to have me arrested because I wouldn't have sex with you?" Kate asked, electrifying the moment.

Deputy Les coughed loudly behind his hand and the dispatcher behind the desk took off his headphone.

"That's not true. You're putting words in her

mouth, McKee. As a citizen, I have a right to file a complaint if—"

Mitch turned to Kate. "Call your father and get him down here. You can use the phone there at the desk."

"Now wait a minute—" Mayor Dealey sputtered. "There's no need to—"

Mitch balanced his hands on his hips and faced the man square on. "Did you think you could have the man's daughter arrested and not have to deal with him?"

"Well, he—"

"Did you think you could try to force Kate into participating in blackmail sex and not have to deal with me?"

"Hi, Daddy," Kate said behind them. "Yes, I know it's late, I—"

Mitch, thinking the entire town wasn't worth the bricks it had taken to build it, stepped over to Kate and put his hand out for the receiver. She'd apologized enough in the past week.

"I woke the baby," she said as she handed it over.

"Hello, Mr. Sutherland?" Mitch said loudly, hoping he might wake up the baby's neighbors as well. "This is Mitch McKee. Your daughter—" he looked at Kate "—Katherine has been arrested for assault. You'd better get down here to the courthouse. I'll expect you in thirty minutes."

KATE'S FATHER arrived in twenty minutes. Mitch decided he would have paid a month's salary to see the look on the mayor's face when he was summoned by

Terry Sutherland into one of the interrogation rooms for a "meeting." Turns out he would be able to see that look any time he needed a good laugh, courtesy of the video camera. He didn't bother to stop Deputy Les and the night dispatcher from watching the monitor. It was enough for him to sit in his office with Kate and hear the occasional shout from down the hall.

"Well, it looks like you have your daddy's complete attention now," Mitch said, thinking that Kate had gotten what she wanted.

"Guess so," she answered absently. She didn't seem very happy about it.

He moved around his desk and approached where she sat in a chair. Squatting down, he looked up at her. "You, okay?"

"I think I just realized I hate this town," she said with a sigh. Then she looked deeply into his eyes and brought one hand up to touch his face. "The best people in it are Julie, and Cal, maybe my sister...and certainly you. I wanted to spend tonight with you, to make it special. You've always been—"

The door to Mitch's office opened and banged against the wall before Terry Sutherland charged through the doorway. "If John Dealey *dares* to take any more legal action against a Sutherland, I'll have him run out of town."

Mitch straightened and faced Kate's father. "Has he withdrawn the complaint then?" he asked.

"I made him tear it up in front of your two deputies. As far as I'm concerned, it's been handled." Then

Mr. Sutherland looked from Mitch to his daughter. "I believe we need to talk, Kate."

Mitch nodded. "You can use my office." He met Kate's gaze before he moved, looking to gauge her mood, but she seemed empty of any emotion. Whatever happened, he couldn't protect her now.

Kate watched Mitch walk through the door then pull it closed behind him. The office seemed bigger without him in it, and more empty.

She was contemplating how empty her life might be without him when her father did something amazing. Instead of sitting behind Mitch's desk, he rolled the leather executive chair around until it faced the chair she was sitting in. Her traitorous mind recognized that if he'd done something as simple as giving her his entire attention a week ago, everything would have been different.

Of course, then she might not have found Mitch...

Kate was close enough to notice the skin on her father's face was mottled pink, from anger or some other emotion. "Kate," he began, then stalled. "I, uh... You don't have to worry about John Dealey. As you heard, I've taken care of that."

"Did he tell you what I—"

"I believe so." Her father stopped her. "And if there's more, I'd rather not know."

As hard as her behavior would be to talk about, she still wasn't sure whether he didn't want to hear because of her discomfort, or his own.

Her father cleared his throat and straightened his back. "I'm very sorry I haven't done better by you, but what's passed is past. I think the best thing for all concerned is for you to go back to your life in San Francisco."

Kate's vision blurred from unwanted tears. The hard-won apology she'd received didn't change a thing. *What's passed is past.* He wanted her to leave and not cause any more trouble in his town. The lump of defeat in her throat blocked any glib reply.

"I know that you and Mitch McKee—"

"Why?" Her voice broke but she forced out the word. "Why can't we be a family?"

Her father looked down at his clasped hands until Kate thought he'd decided not to answer. But just as she'd given up, he drew in a huge breath and met her gaze.

"We can't be a family," he said. "Susan is still a little insecure about her—about our marriage. She's only a few years older than you are... We can't, that's all." He looked her in the eye like a businessman then. "I have provided for you and your sister in my will. You don't have to worry about being disinherited."

Kate faced her father and felt that, for the first time, he'd told her the truth.

"I don't care about the money," she said. And she didn't.

"I know." Her father patted her hand briefly, before going on. "Now, about Mitch. I hope you aren't considering staying in Chapel because of him. Not that he isn't a good man." At lightning speed, her father returned to his natural-born, better-than-you persona. "He isn't the right kind of man for you."

Kate wanted to disagree about Mitch, but she knew she couldn't disagree about staying in Chapel. That was not an option. She realized she'd heard all the truth and advice she needed, or would get, from her father.

She stood up. "Don't worry, Daddy. I'll be on that plane tomorrow." She kissed his cheek and said, "Thank you. Goodbye."

MITCH DROVE HER back to the resort. Not ready to talk yet, after the uproar of the evening, Kate spent the drive looking out the window of Mitch's four-by-four, watching the streets of Chapel go by.

It would be the last time she'd see them.

He walked her from his truck to her room like a hired bodyguard. At the courthouse, he'd removed his jacket and tie and had rolled up the sleeves of his dress shirt. But still, no one would mistake him for anything but a world of trouble if provoked.

He waited for her to unlock the door, then stood there in the hallway with the posture of a stranger not sure of his welcome.

Again, without words, Kate reached for his hand and led him inside.

"I want to say goodbye like an adult," he said. He closed the door behind him but remained stiffly aloof.

Kate turned and stepped into his arms. "I don't want to say goodbye at all, not now, not yet," she said. His hands slid up her back. She raised her chin until her lips were close to his ear. "I want to do what we've been wanting to do the entire evening. Please stay."

She could feel the muscles in his arms clench without completely relaxing.

"Don't ask me to drive you to the airport," he said, as if she could understand the male logic of his words. He must know she'd agree to anything at this point, but he wasn't going to ask.

The threat of tears tightened her throat. "It's a deal," she whispered. *Now, please make me forget I'm leaving you.*

Mitch bent and lifted her in his arms. He carried her to the bed and placed her gently on the mattress. He helped her out of her clothes and shrugged out of his own. No hurry, but without the playfulness as well. Mitch was as deadly serious as Kate had ever seen him and the cause nearly broke her heart.

As he slid onto the sheets with her, Kate had to use every bit of her control not to cling to him and cry. There would be more than enough time for tears when she was alone in her apartment, three thousand miles from Chapel, Tennessee, and a world away from the man she loved.

"WELL, THAT'S EVERYTHING," Kate said as Julie slipped an arm around her and they walked toward the car. "I've called my sister, left a message for my father, I—"

"Maybe you should try Mitch one more time," Julie suggested gently.

Kate blinked away the tears of realization that she might never see some of the people in Chapel she loved ever again. "No. I can't," she said. "We said our goodbye."

That wasn't precisely true. Their bodies had said goodbye, but the words, the words had been too hard. Mitch had loved her as though she meant everything to him, then he'd held her until she'd fallen asleep. When she opened her eyes to the morning light, however, he was already gone.

"If I don't get on the road, I'll really start to boo-hoo and Randy will have to drive." She signaled the young man who worked for Ramey, and who would be driving with her to the airport, to get in the passenger side of the Mercedes.

Kate turned to her friend. "I love ya, kiddo. You take care of that baby now, you hear?"

Julie already had tear tracks on her face but she tried to smile. They both knew Kate would not be back to visit. "Don't worry. Cal will look out for the two of us," Julie said, "Maybe all three of us will come visit you in California."

"I hope so," Kate said, although Julie's innocent words had sent a swordlike thrust of pain through her. *Cal will look out for the two of us.* Just as Mitch had said, Cal was Julie's anchor.

And I'm still out here twisting in the wind.

With one final hug, Kate opened the Mercedes' door and slid into the driver's seat, every atom of her being already missing Mitch and wondering where he'd gone.

"WELL, AT LEAST you didn't get completely stupid," Mitch said to no one in particular. Seated in his favorite lawn chair, on his favorite dock, on his favorite lake—a six-pack of beer dangling from a rope to cool in the lake water—Mitch was congratulating himself. Toasting the wind with Miller Lite.

He wasn't really in the mood to celebrate, yet. He'd only had seven beers so far, but he'd get there. He had to. Because Kate's plane was long gone on its way to the farthest possible destination from Chapel. And he'd never told her he loved her.

It didn't even faze him when Cal's truck rumbled up the gravel road and came to a stop near the cabin. Except to inspire him to pull the beer dangling from the rope up so that he could offer Cal one.

As Cal pulled up another chair and accepted the beer, Mitch held his up for a real toast.

"I quit my job," he announced. "They said I had to give them a month to find another candidate but they're gonna have to come up here and get me."

"You're drunk," Cal said calmly before taking a swig of his beer.

"I'm trying like hell," Mitch agreed and the reason for it drifted a little too close, sharpening the pain he was trying to outrun. He shifted in another direction, stretching his legs out and crossing his ankles like a man of leisure. "I'm gonna grow a beard and live up here in the woods," Mitch proclaimed as if he'd hit on a real goal for his life.

"She tried to call you—"

"Don't!" Mitch ordered. "I can't— Dammit!"

Wanting to hit something, anything, he did the only thing at hand. He threw the half-finished can of beer as hard as he could. As it splashed then disappeared into the water, he covered his eyes with his hands. "Just kill me now. I can't stand this."

He drew in a calming breath, forcing the idea that he'd never see Kate again further and further back in his mind. He had to stand it. He'd known she was trouble when he first saw her again, sitting on that car in a ditch full of mud. He just hadn't known how much losing her would hurt. The saddest part, the really sick part, in his opinion, was that he'd do it all over again, in a heartbeat, if he ever got the chance.

Grateful for Cal's silence, Mitch rubbed his face and sat back to stare out over the lake. She was gone. He had lived through it. He'd get over it.

"So, did you really quit your job?" Cal asked.

15

IT HAD ONLY TAKEN a three-hour flight for Kate to want to see Mitch beyond sanity. Upon arrival at her apartment in the Mission District, it had taken a six-minute phone call to find out he'd moved to the cabin at the lake. One of the few places he'd be without a phone. It had taken a month to get over the hurt that he, in effect, had no intention of talking to her anytime soon. That it had to be all or nothing.

It took six weeks to find out she was pregnant.

Sitting in her bathroom on a foggy Saturday morning, looking at that little blue line, she felt a rightness about it. Some part of her must have known that she and Mitch had made a baby, probably that first day at the lake. Now she had to decide what to do about the future. She and Mitch had real things to discuss at this point, not just I miss you, wish you were here. She'd talk to him about this baby if she had to fly back to Chapel to do it.

She was *not* going to be a single mother—not unless Mitch had an insurmountable reason why they shouldn't try to make a family. After all, they had a head start. And, it wasn't like they'd made this baby without love. Her heart had been involved, and even though Mitch hadn't said it, his must have been as well.

Kate's mind drifted to having someone to come home to, to depend on when the rest of the world got crazy. An anchor, just as Mitch advised. Well, she thought, it's time for him to put up, or shut up. And it's time for us to both leave the past in Chapel, and start a new life.

Kate Sutherland went to the telephone. She was going to propose to the biggest troublemaker in Chapel, Tennessee. The biggest one besides herself, that is.

She was going to ask Mitch McKee to marry her.

"YOU SHOULDN'T be doing this, Julie," Mitch said as she fussed around his place setting. "You look about ready to pop any minute." Julie and Cal had invited him into town for a home-cooked meal, and since he hadn't seen Julie in a couple of weeks, the progression of her pregnancy took him by surprise.

"Oh, stop it! I'm just fine. I've got a few more weeks to go," Julie replied. "And you can't stay up there in the hills eating beef jerky and drinking beer all the time." She stared at his beard for thirty seconds. "A little hair on your face doesn't cover the fact that you've lost weight."

Mitch looked at Cal for support, but he just shrugged. He brought his attention back to Julie. "Well, you seem a little jumpy and it's making me nervous."

"Me, nervous?" Julie asked, pressing a hand to her

extended belly. "I'm just—" She glanced at Cal looking at a loss for words.

"Energetic," Cal said, as if that explained the universe of Julie.

Mitch gave up. He shook his head and was about to change the subject when a car pulled into the drive. Cal remained seated but Julie headed for the door like a shot.

"It's a police car," Julie said.

A bad feeling ran up Mitch's spine. After Julie's strange behavior, he wondered if she'd had some premonition of doom. Pregnant women were as mysterious as fortune tellers to him. But, he reasoned, he didn't have anyone to worry about. His best friends were in the room with him, and Kate...Kate was safe in San Francisco. Safe. How would he know if she was safe or not?

After a smart knock on the door, Julie swung it open and welcomed Deputy Arnold into the dining room. Cal stood up then. "What's the problem, Deputy?"

The deputy looked at Mitch. "I have an emergency radio call for the chief—I mean, Mr. McKee," he said.

The oddest thing happened then. Mitch reached for the portable radio and, as he did so, he glanced at Julie. She was smiling.

Thinking the whole world seemed to be tilting toward crazy, Mitch spoke into the radio.

"This is Mitch McKee."

"Chief? Deputy Les here. You remember a while back when Miz Sutherland put her car in a ditch?"

Mitch's heart began to beat like it wanted out of his chest. "Yeah, Les. I remember."

"Well, sir. She's done it again. She's—"

"Where?"

"Ravenswood Road, just outside the city limits. I—"

Without waiting to hear more, Mitch handed the radio back to the deputy. "I hope you're not parked behind my truck," he warned as he walked past him.

"No, sir."

"Mitch, wait!" Julie ordered. Then she reached up to hug him. "Don't screw it up," she whispered.

PUFFS OF DUST rose around Mitch's tires in the late afternoon light when he brought his truck to a halt near Deputy Les's patrol car. Kate watched as the deputy, who'd already said goodbye to her, nodded to Mitch then got into his patrol car and pulled away. That left her and Mitch, alone on the side of the road, just outside the city of their beginning and hopefully not their ending.

The man walking toward her looked like a stranger. Thinner than he'd been and wearing a sinister-looking dark beard, he could have been mistaken for an outlaw rather than the chief of police. But then she'd heard he quit his job. His steps were deliberate and unhurried, which caused another rush of nervousness in Kate. What if he didn't love her, didn't want her or their baby?

But when he got close enough for her to see his

eyes, she knew. He was glad to see her. Very glad. She couldn't help but smile.

"You didn't make it all the way in the ditch this time," he commented, since her car was simply parked on the shoulder.

"I didn't want to wreck this one," she admitted. "It's a rental."

For a brief, wonderful moment, she thought he was going to hug her but instead he slipped his hands into his pockets. "How've you been?" he asked.

"Terrible," she admitted. "Until just recently, that is." She gave him her best frown. "Why didn't you call me?"

"I, uh—" He glanced away from her, down the length of the road. When he returned his gaze to hers, he looked like a man who'd lost his soul. "I told you. I'm not good at goodbyes. Saying them over and over won't make me any better at it."

Kate walked toward him then and bracketed his bearded face with her hands. "Do you love me, Mitch McKee?"

Mitch drew in a long, slow breath, then let it out. "You know I do," he said. He brought his hands up and circled her wrists. "I think I have since high school."

Trying not to smile, Kate took one of his large hands and pressed it to her still flat belly. "Remember that day at the lake when you said we should act like seventeen-year-olds?"

He nodded.

"Well, you've gone and got me pregnant." Before

he could speak, she stepped closer and kissed him. "If you'd done that back in high school, we'd have a family by now."

Mitch was sure he was dreaming. He had to be. The woman he loved was in his arms, and the fantasy of her having his baby was almost a reality.

"If I'm dead and in heaven, don't tell me," he said as he looked into Kate's sparkling blue eyes. The sun had sent out a final shaft of golden light just for them it seemed. Her hair looked like fire and, for a second, he prayed that their daughter would be a fiery wild girl just like her mother.

"Will you do the right thing and marry me?" Kate asked. "I think this baby and I are in the market for an anchor."

"You haven't said you love me," Mitch informed her.

"You know what you said about loving since high school?" She gazed into his eyes. "I loved you first."

Unable to wait any longer, Mitch kissed her like a madman, then like a lover, then like an expectant father.

"What will your daddy say?" Mitch asked. Although he didn't care, he needed to know if Kate did.

"Oh, that's the one stipulation to this proposal," Kate said in a businesslike manner, not unlike her father's. "This baby and I aren't going to set foot in Chapel. You'll have to find a new place to fish—in California."

"Not a problem."

_____ Epilogue _____

THEY'D BEEN HALFWAY through a three-day fishing trip at their cabin in the mountains when Kate went into labor. Actually, they'd been in the middle of Lake Shasta in a boat when her water broke.

Kate had had the nerve to make a joke about water, water, everywhere before looking at him with wide eyes, and saying, "It's time." She hadn't seemed afraid, more like ready.

Mitch hadn't been so sanguine. He trusted Kate's judgment, but he also knew she'd never had a baby before so it was up to him to be the serious party.

With calm detachment, he dropped his string of newly caught fish over the side along with the unused bait, then started the engine to head for shore.

He'd been the transportation man. He drove the boat, the car, the wheelchair. He got her to the hospital in a little over an hour and a half, then spent the next twelve hours worrying, coaching and praying.

Then, finally, he held his baby daughter in his trembling hands. Mitch McKee, the hellion of Chapel, Tennessee, looked from the perfect face of his angelic daughter to the proud and beautiful face of his angelic wife, and said the first thing that came into his dazed mind.

"She's grounded until she's twenty-one."

HARLEQUIN®

Temptation

COMING NEXT MONTH

#785 MOONLIGHTING Heather MacAllister
Sweet Talkin' Guys

Amber Madison had always had a weakness for sweet-talkin'
Logan Van Dell. Years ago he'd even charmed her into running
away with him—then he'd left her to go on alone. Now Amber is
home, and Logan's just as irresistible. During their moonlight
trysts, Amber can't help falling for him all over again. But will
Logan still be around when the sun comes up?

#786 SAWYER Lori Foster
The Buckhorn Brothers, Bk. 1

The day Honey Malone—fleeing from a dangerous predator—
drove her car into a lake, she found herself up to her neck in
gorgeous men! After Sawyer Hudson—Buckhorn's only doctor—
and his three bachelor brothers nursed her through her injuries,
she tried to leave. But she hadn't bargained on the stubborn
protectiveness of the Buckhorn Brothers.

#787 TOO HOT TO SLEEP Stephanie Bond
Blaze

Georgia Adams couldn't sleep…and it wasn't because of the local
heat wave. She had a lukewarm boyfriend, a nonexistent love
life…and she was frustrated, *really* frustrated. Deciding to heat
things up, she phoned her boyfriend for a little phone
flirtation…and a lot more. Her bold experiment was wildly
successful. Only, Georgia didn't realize she'd dialed the wrong
number….

#788 BOONE'S BOUNTY Vicki Lewis Thompson
Three Cowboys & A Baby

Shelby McFarland and her three-year-old nephew, Josh, were on
the run. When a snowstorm left them stranded, Shelby thought
the game was over…until a strong, sexy cowboy rescued them.
Boone Connor made Shelby feel safe, protected—and very, very
desired. They'd make a perfect family—only, Boone already had a
baby….

CNM0500